Ciao, Amore Mio

Ciao, Amore Mio

The Tale of Gabby and Gio
An Italian Discovery

J.A. Marz

Printed in the United States of America
Published in Hellertown, PA
Cover design by Nancy McLaughlin
Library of Congress Control Number 2024925988
ISBN 979-8-89420-035-4
"Va, Pensiero" (Italian: [ˈva penˈsjɛːro]), is a chorus from the opera Nabucco (1842) by Giuseppe Verdi. Reference to Zucchero and Pavarotti is from a live concert staged in Modena, Italy "Pavarotti & Friends" For the Children of Liberia June 9, 1998.

For more information, reprint permissions, or to place bulk orders, contact the author at Jmarz40@gmail.com or the publisher at Jennifer@BrightCommunications.net.

To all those on the journey to self-discovery:
The road is paved like the Roman Appian
Way—bumpy. Embrace the ride, nurture it, and
smooth it out for others.

Chapter 1

The Soul of Life

Gio never expected Gabby's presence to be so strong and close. Yet fate had different intentions.

A celebration was underway with several hundred guests enjoying food and wine on the terrace at one of Gabby's most cherished spots—the Grand Hotel Timeo in Taormina, Sicily. Perched high atop a hill along the Via Teatro Greco, the location bordered the ancient outdoor theater. With breathtaking panoramic views of the Sicilian coastline, it embodied luxury in a town boasting annals dating back to the fifth century, if not earlier.

The Grand Timeo was undeniably grand and steeped in history. Old yet elegant, the hotel always welcomed guests to indulge in Sicilian splendor for a few days.

Late September marked the ideal time to visit the island, too. The warm climate coaxed bougainvillea into bloom. The lush gardens surrounding the hotel were vibrant, and a sweet floral scent filled the air. Cool nights signaled the start of the evening walk tradition, a *passeggiata* after the stifling heat dissipated and tourists had long gone.

As Zucchero and Pavarotti serenaded the atmosphere with their enchanting tune,

"Va' pensiero, sull'ali dorate...
Cross the mountains and fly
Over the oceans.
Reach the land, find the place where all children go
Every night after listening to this lullaby..."

The majestic sight of Mount Etna smoking in the distance was rivaled by only one other captivating image in Gio's room: Gabriella Buca Rosetti was a vision of beauty. Her brown hair cascaded around strong shoulders, while her piercing blue eyes set fire to ice.

Known affectionately as Gabby, she turned heads wherever she went. Her witnessed rare beauty left grown men speechless and sent young Italian boys to the privacy of self-pleasure. Gabby was exceptional, intelligent, talented, full of life, and strikingly beautiful—with attentive curves, olive skin, long legs leading to a shaped posterior, thin ruby lips, and the voice of an angel.

Gabby was a killer of hearts. And she always had a way of melting Gio's.

"Hey, Babe," came a sudden, bewitching siren. "What are you staring at, Gio?"

"Your beauty into my soul," he said aloud with his eyes closed. "I want to remember it forever."

And now, Giovanni Maranzzano III—Gio Marzo for short, a fourth generation of Italian immigrants from Naples—was about to attend a gathering filled with people he had long neglected, with the most beautiful woman imaginable, yet he couldn't help but feel he had fucked it all up.

Chapter 2

The Beginning

Gabby and Gio's story started in the late summer of 2021 in San Gimignano, a charming town where the morning mist of the Val d'Elsa caresses the olive groves and grape vineyards of the Tuscan countryside. Later each evening, the sunsets bathe the sky in shades of gold and pink.

San Gimi is a medieval town between Florence and Siena. Here, time appears to pause, allowing people to enjoy life's simple pleasures—except during the bustling tourist season when they're lined three deep in Gelateria Dondoli waiting for the world's best gelato.

Gio was in San Gimi on assignment, finishing a travel piece about the region's hidden gems—its history and fortress of towers, the ancient groves, and the local vineyards producing some of Italy's finest olive oil and wines.

Gabby was visiting the area alone for a much-needed escape from the workload of her family's vineyard. After her father's recent passing, she was thrust into running the operations of the estate—La Terre Felice—in central Italy, but she was uncertain if she was prepared to join her mother, Antoinette, in managing that significant responsibility. The property represented the Rosetti family's legacy, yet it also presented a significant burden. Gabby had come to San Gimi for clarity, hoping the peaceful nights would provide time for reflection and result in some answers. She was living life as an artist and art historian while serving as the keeper of the Rosetti estate archives for her parents. She hadn't anticipated taking on the ownership so soon.

One September evening, Gabby's path crossed with Gio's at a small, family-owned trattoria. Gio sat at a corner table, scribbling notes in his worn leather journal while typing on his laptop. Gabby sat at an opposite corner, lost in thought, her mind racing to address unanswered questions about the future of her family's vineyard.

The restaurant's owner, a friendly older woman named Rosa, who had welcomed Gabby to the trattoria since she was a child, played matchmaker.

"Gabriella, come here, Cara," Rosa called, waving her over to Gio's table. "You must meet this young man. He's a writer traveling the world, but tonight he's here with us."

Gabby hesitated, but Rosa was persistent, and soon she found herself seated across from Gio. He glanced up from his journal, their intense gazes locking, and for a moment, they both sensed a spark—a connection neither could quite put into words.

"You're a writer?" Gabby asked, breaking the silence.

Gio smiled as he closed his laptop. "Absolutely! I travel a lot and enjoy writing about the destinations I explore, the people I encounter, and the often-overlooked stories that deserve to be shared. And you?"

Gabby shrugged, a small smile playing on her lips. "I'm sorry. This might be odd to share when we just met, but my brain is so preoccupied with something: My father recently passed away, and I just inherited my family's vineyard, but I'm not sure running it is the path I want to take. I'm trying to make sense of everything, I suppose."

Gio's curiosity was piqued. Gabby's story was fascinating and looking at her was like witnessing the beauty of the Italian Renaissance. She was stunning. "A vineyard? Sounds incredible. But it must be a lot of pressure, carrying on a legacy, I imagine."

Gabby nodded, surprised at how easily Gio seemed to understand her inner conflict. "We own groves of ancient olive trees and vineyards that require year-round management and timely harvesting. Managing it all is a more-than-full-time job—far too much for my mother to oversee by herself," she explained.

Despite Gabby's radiant beauty, she suffered from a chronic autoimmune disease that manifested in subtle yet debilitating ways. On good days, she glowed and was full of life, with her laughter echoing through the vineyards.

However, during flare-ups, joint pain, fatigue, and breathing difficulties were triggered to knock Gabby down. Her breathing became labored and shallow, and each step required visible effort. The vibrant energy surrounding her diminished, replaced by an aura of quiet struggle.

Gabby's illness started when she was a young child. Most doctors at the time didn't understand how lifestyle and environmental factors influenced chronic health issues. When Gabby got sick, her immune system took longer to fight off infection and illness.

The chronic health issue was a constant undercurrent in Gabby's life, and it influenced every decision she made. It also added complexity to any blooming romantic relationship.

That evening, Gabby and Gio talked for hours, sharing their dreams, fears, and hopes, as they drank a few carafes of the local Vernaccia wine. Gio told Gabby about his love for the open road, the thrill of hustling fellow golfers as a sideline while discovering new places, and the freedom of his nomadic lifestyle.

"I'm facing such a big decision," Gabby said. "La Terre Felice is beautiful—its name literally means 'the happy land.' I want to honor my father and our family and make the estate even better.

Yet I also want a life of my own. The question is: Can I do both?"

Rosa, relishing her job as matchmaker, was in no hurry to see Gabby and Gio leave her cozy oasis. But, as the evening wore on, Gabby and Gio left the trattoria, then walked the quiet Via San Giovanni to Piazza della Cisterna for a tasty gelato, which they enjoyed while sitting on the steps of the historic Santa Maria Assunta church in Piazza del Duomo. The sounds of crickets and muted laughter offered a soothing backdrop for their ongoing conversation.

Gabby's warmth, kindness, and charismatic strength, which seemed to radiate from her, captivated Gio. She spoke with an angelic yet confident tone, often using vivid descriptions to convey her passion for life and the land she loves.

"I was raised to appreciate a working farm and the land that provided bountiful nourishment for our village," she said. "It's given me a sense of belonging and an understanding of what *familia* means."

Gabby was drawn to Gio's zest for life, his pioneering spirit, and how he viewed the world with a writer's eye—always looking for uniqueness in the everyday.

"People always have a story to tell," Gio added. "I'm not afraid to explore what makes a place, an event, or a person special. I'm passionate about that calling."

Chapter 3

Roots of Contrast

Gio Marzo's roots traced back to Caivano, Italy, which today is part of the industrial waste dump of the Campania region. His great-grandfather Giovanni emigrated to America more than a century ago as a steerage passenger on a steamer from the Port of Naples across the Atlantic to Ellis Island.

Giovanni was a crafted stone mason, and he helped to build many beautiful churches and homes with large cut stones that are still standing tall today in Pennsylvania and New Jersey. Cutting stone was hard work, and Giovanni's hands were as rough as the rocks he shaped.

Gio's aura was a fourth generation of the same blood. Hard-edged and rough with a sting, he was the antithesis of Gabby's peaceful inner strength. In direct contrast to the charm of the Tuscan hillside, Naples evoked raw, gritty, and dangerous. This transcended its residents, family descendants, and way of life. A man with an air of mystery and an insatiable desire to explore, Gio III was born in America and grew up in the Northeastern United States.

Gio's father abandoned the family early in Gio's life. So he was raised by his mother, Isabella, and grandmother, Madeline. Both of these women of elegance and strength aimed to provide the best for young Gio.

Like many Italian-American boys growing up in close-knit neighborhoods, Gio as the male child was everything. He was adored and spoiled by his grandmother, who always reminded him "to be good for Nonna."

In comparison to the loving treatment Gio received at home, outside of home, Gio was ridiculed in mixed company because of his ethnicity. He hated being Italian because other kids always made fun of him.

Yet Gio was a good student. He studied hard and graduated from one of the top journalism schools on the East Coast. Then he bought a one-way ticket to Europe.

Restless as a boy and now a grown man, Gio had an affinity for golf. He could hustle the best of them, which set him on a path to traverse the globe with an addictive appetite for adventure, Italy, and women.

Gio's rugged, sophisticated appearance was one of tailored clothes leaning into an appreciation for the finer things in life. His well-worn leather jacket was lined with reminders of countless escapades and journeys. A perpetual five o'clock shadow and piercing hazel eyes held the secrets of Gio's heritage and every place traveled. His tousled chestnut hair often caught the sunlight as he moved from one destination to another, a traveler with no fixed address.

Gio wore a constant half-smile, a testament to the many beautiful women he encountered in his travels and the pros he hustled playing golf. While he didn't win them all, money lost in a game was the price of valuable insight gained for the next time. All were chapters in the collection of Gio's nomadic life story.

As a scribe, Gio's words transported readers to far-off lands. Each sentence dripped with vivid colors, exquisite fragrances, textured landscapes, and the rich history of places experienced. His prose was a captivating blend of eloquence and raw, unfiltered emotion—trademarks of a man who reveled in the joy of rooted tradition and real discovery.

His dialogue was marked by its warmth and wit. He spoke with a reflective tone, revealing glimpses of an inner turmoil just beneath light-hearted banter. His words carried the weight of someone accustomed to looking outward into the world, yet also contemplative about life's deeper meanings.

Gio was more than a wordsmith. As a golfer, he challenged local pros on the most obscure courses, turning every game into a betting narrative. His weathered clubs hid tales of fairways conquered, opponents outplayed, and money won—and lost.

For all Gio's exploits, his adventurous exterior obscured his softer side. A hopeless romantic chasing dreams and carnal desires across the globe, he always found beauty in the connections made along his journey.

Each lover Gio encountered wrote a chapter in the epic novel of his life. Each woman became a testament to the transient nature of romance and self-discovery in a world moving at warp speed. Gio lived in perpetual motion, a symphony of experiences composed of the places he visited and the people he befriended on his ceaseless quest for the next great adventure.

Yet watching the years, Gio realized something was missing. Family had rarely been part of his adult life, and he yearned for a sense of belonging.

Chapter 4

The Connection

Sure enough after meeting Gabby in San Gimi, Gio remained in the area for weeks, making excuses to hang out with her.

As autumn progressed, and the busy harvest season ended, Gabby and Gio were able to move about freely throughout the countryside. Crisp mornings gave way to warm October sunshine—perfect for exploring the region—while cool evenings allowed them to savor the best food in outdoor cafes. Gabby and Gio explored the region, climbing neighboring villages built into the tops of hills, like Montepulciano, Assisi, and Pienza. They sampled wines in the vineyards, ate fig-stuffed tortellini along Ruga Piana in Cortona, and spent long afternoons talking, talking, and more talking under that famous Tuscan sun.

As Gabby and Gio's travels uncovered and discovered more, they found the crazy array of saints' *festas* that populate the Italian calendar. All are living expressions of local values, as townsfolk celebrate a religious saint with music, dance, and food.

Catholicism is foundational in Italy. Each town reveres the Madonna Mary with makeshift shrines cut into the sides of buildings. Those tiny enclaves honor devotion with fresh flowers placed and lighted candles daily.

Every community worships in its church or cathedral, too. Gio and Gabby's emotional experience of visiting religious locations culminated in Assisi, where the Basilica di San Francesco d'Assisi adorns a prime corner of the square to honor its patron, Saint Francis. These experiences deepened Gio and Gabby's connection, and soon they were inseparable.

One evening in early November, as Gabby and Gio sat on the terrace of Gabby's temporary home in San Gimi, watching the stars in the night sky, Gio turned to her with a sober expression. "Bella, I've never felt this way before. I've always been so focused on traveling and writing, but with you… I see a different life—one that doesn't involve moving, but staying in one place, building something real."

Gabby's heart fluttered at his words. She agreed but was afraid to say it, worried it might scare him away. "Me too, Gio," she admitted. "But what if it doesn't work? What if you get restless and want to leave?"

Gio took her hand and looked into her eyes, his gaze steady. "I'm not sure what the future holds for us, but I don't want to lose what we share. Perhaps we can create a life together while still embracing a spirit of adventure. I don't have all the answers, but I'm eager to explore this with you."

Great conversations continued as they grew closer. Gabby talked about La Terre Felice, sharing stories of her childhood, the way her parents had poured their hearts into the estate's vineyard, and her dreams of maybe turning it into something more—an *agriturismo* where people could come to experience the beauty of working the land and the warmth of its people.

The estate's land provided many opportunities, such as planting in early spring, nurturing the produce, observing the ripening of grape vines and olive trees throughout the summer months, tending to the farm animals, and finally experiencing the fall harvest.

Gabby hoped that some of the most memorable times for guests would be when they joined the staff and local villagers in harvesting ripened grapes and stomping them barefooted in the large bins. Even though the processing has advanced today with modern technology, the stomping of the grapes was symbolic of the traditions passed down through generations.

Gio listened, fascinated by Gabby's vision, and he saw how he might fit into that life. He imagined himself writing from a small room overlooking the vineyard, helping Gabby with the guests, and finding inspiration in the rhythms of traditional Italian life.

Gio's passion for travel and the freedom it offered was integral to him, just as the ground and earth of La Terre Felice were for Gabby. They each understood life together would involve compromise, and they both were unsure how it would unfold.

Despite their uncertainties, they couldn't ignore their feelings for one another.

"Gio, would La Terre Felice excite your sense of adventure?" Gabby questioned. "It might be the opportunity for us to work together."

Gio, always cautious and guarded, looked into Gabby's eyes and surprised her with his response. "You know, I've traveled the world searching for a certain, grounded identity," he said. "This sounds extraordinary, so Italian. I love it. I'm touched by your offer to include me in your plans."

Within days, Gio returned with Gabby to La Terre Felice, where they spent the next few months exploring each other physically and collaborating on various projects. Gio's keen eye for travel destinations and his talent to describe them provided the *agriturismo* with a new brand identity that could be sold with words to adventurous travel seekers worldwide.

It was a joyful time for both of them. Gio found fresh inspiration in the vineyard's serene beauty, while Gabby felt a deep sense of fulfillment in sharing her family's legacy with visitors—and of course Gio. The visit helped them envision a future where they could harmonize their love with their passions.

"I want to write about this place," Gio said. "La Terre Felice has a spirit, and the stories of the people who visit and work here would be captivating. An article—even a book about the Rosetti family would be a legacy for sure."

Gabby had been advancing her idea of expanding the vineyard into a flourishing *agriturismo* to attract guests from around the globe. She cherished this time working side-by-side with her mother and her team, who had grown to be like family. Gabby and Gio discussed the possibility of traveling together during the off-season winter months, exploring new destinations while still having a place to call home.

But as time passed, the difficulties of merging their lives became clearer. By late winter, Gio's restlessness returned as he was offered well-paying assignments to travel and write. He found it hard to remain in one place for so long—and harder and harder to turn down those choice projects.

On the other hand, each day Gabby felt more anchored in La Terre Felice. Her inner strength was her commitment, and she realized this was where she belonged. "I'm embracing this responsibility, Gio," she said. "La Terre Felice— the *agriturismo*—is my dream. It could be *our* dream."

Gio felt his stomach clench. "*Cazzo*," he replied, harsher than intended.

Over the next few days, their discussions about the future grew more intense, filled with unspoken anxieties and a growing awareness they might not be able to reconcile their differing aspirations.

I don't want to leave, but I can't stay, Gio thought.

I wish I could travel. But I can't abdicate my growing responsibilities here, Gabby reflected.

Yet, even amidst these uncertainties, their relationship deepened. Theirs was a connection built on shared aspirations, respect for each other's talents, and a profound understanding of each other's hearts.

Then Gio was offered a project he couldn't refuse. That evening, he pulled his chair close to Gabby's and said, "Gabby, an international travel company has asked me to do a series of articles on Africa, particularly the North African region. It's an area younger travelers are discovering, and I want to explore why."

"But what happens to us?" Gabby responded. "How do we manage any relationship? How do I keep you with me when your travels take you so far away?"

"I want to promise you that we can communicate regularly, yet these are remote areas without much technology," Gio said. "This job could extend for several months, but know this, Gabriella, you will always be always with me."

When Gio made the difficult choice to leave La Terre Felice for that opportunity, it was bittersweet for them both. They recognized their genuine love, yet they understood they couldn't push each other into lives they were unprepared to embrace. They parted with trust in their hearts.

Chapter 5

Ode to the Vagabond

Gabby's loss of Gio's presence was palpable after he left Italy for a new travel writing assignment in Morocco. Absorbed by the weight of his absence and the void of their complicated relationship, she threw herself into the one thing that could provide solace. She knew that focusing on the property would help distract her from Gio's departure and offer her a sense of purpose.

"Did Gio provide you any means of communicating with him?" Mamma Antoinette asked, concerned for her daughter's happiness, but also trying to stay aligned with the young man Gabby was missing terribly.

"He said he would reach out when possible," Gabby explained. "Gio said it was remote, so I don't expect to hear much while he's adventuring. I'm going to try not to think about it for now. You and I and this place are all we can control right now, Mamma."

While Gio was on assignment, he immersed himself completely in his work—without any communication to Gabby, her family, or anyone—much to the detriment of others.

Always in flux in his travels, Gio's home on wheels was either a sport Fiat or Vespa parked along coastal cliffs, nestled in forest clearings, or tucked away in quiet villages throughout these countries. The one constant in his otherwise wandering personality was to travel light, never knowing when he would need a quick getaway from a storyline—or a woman.

Morocco, a country on the North African continent, is rigged with mystery and terrain uncommon to the average traveler. Gio used his prose to navigate the Straits of Gibraltar as an example of a journey written for any location to make it appeal to the world.

During the next four months, Gabby worked. Each day, she woke before dawn, ready to face the challenges of running a new Tuscan retreat. She walked the five-kilometer-square grounds, ensuring everything was perfect, from the three large olive groves and four acres of grape vines to the neatly trimmed lavender bushes that bordered the farm and its cottages to the tall cypress trees that soldiered the entrance to the rustic stone pathways leading to the vineyards. Gabby was proud to now be the artist of this evolving landscape.

Despite the ache in Gabby's heart from Gio's absence, she still greeted every guest with a warm smile. Her striking looks hid her inner turmoil.

The guests saw her as the heart and soul of the estate, an embodiment of the beauty and charm of Tuscany itself.

Gabby oversaw all details, yet after her father's sudden death, she was not alone in her quest to sustain and enhance La Terre Felice. Her mother was her steadfast partner in this endeavor, with a total commitment to keep her husband's patriarchal spirit alive.

Antoinette, the quintessential Italian Mamma was a warm, welcoming presence. Even though her strong-boned figure had been softened by years of hard work and family love, she still maintained the strength to transform her grief into a revitalized passion for the family's estate.

Antoinette's culinary skills were renowned, and her hands showed the marks of countless hours spent in the kitchen preparing meals that brought people together. She used her experience to grow La Terre Felice's menu into a delightful mix of Mediterranean and Tuscan dishes. She always served plenty of pasta and manicotti—her siren calls to the vagabond Gio—and she took great pride in crafting authentic Italian dishes, drawing from recipes passed down through generations. Consequently, her skill became the culinary soul of La Terre Felice, attracting guests from far and wide, who came for the serene landscapes and the unforgettable meals that told the story of their Italian heritage.

Together, Gabby and Antoinette made a formidable team. Gabby focused on the broader vision, bringing in modern touches and ensuring that La Terre Felice could compete in a changing tourism industry. In contrast, Antoinette preserved the place's warmth and tradition. They broadened the menu, launched cooking classes for tour groups, and even began hosting distinctive dinners that gained popularity with the locals.

Produce from their land during the growing season also served as the centerpiece for a traditional monthly meal for local villagers on a long table in the town square. Fresh pasta, meats, cheeses, and *pesce* along with oven-baked bread, plump tomatoes, and olive oil that evoked peppery nectar, was all topped off with wine for everyone.

Many locals and guests gushed about the meals as the best Italian food they'd ever eaten. Gabby knew Antoinette's cooking was a huge attraction, and she helped her mother make it memorable for everyone.

Although their collaboration faced some challenges, the relationship between mother and daughter deepened the longer they worked together. La Terre Felice thrived through their combined efforts, becoming a beloved destination that honored the past while embracing the future.

Chapter 6

Tuscany and La Terre Felice

Gabby had always been a dreamer, and her aspirations brought her back to the heart of Tuscany, where she worked to establish the charming *agriturismo*.

Nestled in central Italy, the Tuscan region spans from the Tyrrhenian Sea on its western coast to the rugged Apennine Mountains on the east. This region includes historic towns like Florence, Siena, Lucca, Pisa, and San Gimignano, each boasting a rich culture and architectural marvels.

Tuscany is also renowned for its artistic heritage. Renaissance art flourishes in museums and churches throughout its landscape. Crafts and textiles reflect centuries-old techniques passed down through generations and sold in local shops.

Music plays an integral role in Tuscan history. Traditional Italian folk songs can be heard at festivals and gatherings while opera performances captivate audiences in local theaters. Culinary arts shine here, too, with cooking classes and wine tastings galore.

The Tuscan countryside includes a symphony of sensory delights. The air is filled with the fragrant scent of blooming wildflowers and fresh herbs, mingling with the earthy aroma of tilled soil and ancient olive groves.

The rolling hills, adorned with vineyards, stretch as far as any eyeshot distance. Their lush greenery is punctuated by cypress trees standing tall like border sentinels. The distant hum of human energy adds to the serene ambiance, while the occasional tolling of church bells from nearby towns signals a touch of romantic charm.

The region's diverse terrain includes winding country roads lined with stone walls that invite exploration and quaint villages where time seems to stand still. Tourists flock to this part of Italy each year to experience the carefree life for themselves, knowing words could never substitute for being there.

La Terre Felice, Gabby's inherited estate, laid at the heart of this idyllic landscape surrounded by Tuscany's agricultural bounty. The property featured a blend of rustic charm and modern amenities, with restored stone buildings and terracotta roofs encircled by olive groves, grape vines, and lush decorative plantings. Visitors to La Terre Felice explored its scenic landscapes and enjoyed its cozy accommodations that had been converted from historic farmhouses and barns.

The main house of La Terre Felice was a residence for Gabby and Antoinette and the estate's administrative center, while guests stayed in six charming cottages. The property also included covered outdoor dining areas, gardens, a swimming pool, and outdoor venues spaces for weddings and festivals. The grounds were punctuated by vegetable and flower gardens and encircled by olive groves and vineyards.

The villa estate was vast, and drawing from Gabby's family's resources and keen intuition, she transformed this Tuscan gem into a haven of beauty, tranquility, and creativity. The experience for travelers mimicked going back in time to their youth—to a simpler way of living. A slower pace without the use of a cellphone or computer inspired an open mind to absorb life's visual and tactile experiences. This was La Terre Felice's secret sauce, and Gabby kept it simmering on the fire.

Caring for the property also offered Gabby a respite from thinking about Gio every minute of every day. She poured herself into the demands of the business and working farm and wondered what that nomad was up to any day.

Resilient and determined, Gabby shaped her life by the joys and sorrows of her past. Raised in a family that provided everything and living close to Florence, the arts and historical significance of the Italian Renaissance were constants in her life. Educated in the finest schools and academically brilliant had made her father gush at every chance.

Gabby had adored her father, Antonio, who was the backbone of their family. Their estate was more than a business. It was a sanctuary where Antonio had dedicated his life to highlighting the beauty of central Italy and the essence of true hospitality. He was a beacon in the village community often sought for his historical knowledge. His booming voice was quick with an engaging wit and sage advice to anyone within earshot.

When Antonio had held weekly confabs with the locals, his favorite saying echoed throughout the village, "Life's like tending an olive tree. You need to have patience, care, and a bit of faith in the soil. The fruits only come after you've put in the work."

Gabby had admired her father's passion and commitment. From a young age, she participated in the daily operations of the vineyard, gaining direct experience and forming strong bonds with both the land and its visitors. Her father's dream had been to hand over La Terre Felice to Gabby when ready, confident that she already shared his love for the place.

However, tragedy struck when Antonio died suddenly. His heart gave out one day in the fields. Antonio's death left an emptiness in Gabby's life and also in the operation of La Terre Felice. The responsibility of managing the property fell onto Gabby and Antoinette, a weight she never anticipated so soon but was resolute in bearing.

Despite the sorrow and the daunting obstacles, Gabby vowed not to let her father's dream fade away. She drove herself into work even more to honor his heritage.

As time went on in the months after her father's passing, Gabby updated the estate into an *agriturismo*, turning older buildings and barns into guest accommodations that included both modern amenities and rustic charm, while incorporating hands-on guest participation in working the land and preparing meals for visitors.

Gabby's rich experience in the arts enabled her to showcase the heritage of the estate using its history as a foundation for telling the story of La Terre Felice. Maintaining her family home's ambiance was all about welcoming guests into the essence of Tuscany and Italian life. Gabby's unwavering dedication to La Terre Felice fueled her passion, even while she dealt with personal challenges, including her health, which became a focal point after Antonio's death. The *agriturismo* represented much more to her now. It was a means to honor her father's memory and continue alongside her mother to secure her birthright.

Chapter 7

A Legacy Preserved

By early spring, strong-willed Gabby immersed herself in the agrarian rhythms of La Terre Felice, collaborating with their staff to cultivate the olive trees and grapevines.

Antonio had always been the expert, and immediately after his death, Gabby delegated more work, letting the staff manage it, while she focused on adding the agritourism aspects to the estate. Now, with her heart aching from Gio, the earth became her therapy. She found solace in the soil, a quiet connection to her father, and a reminder of the legacy she was trying to preserve.

Occasionally, Gio would call when he located cell service, and they would spend most of their time updating each other on their work. Even though Gabby desperately wanted to know when Gio would return, she didn't ask. Instead, she focused on the improvements she was making to the estate—with the help of her staff.

La Terre Felice's staff were more than hired hands. They were skilled, talented employees who became extended family. They were invested in supporting the Rosettis, and now they were eager to help with the success of the *agriturismo*.

Like casting a movie, the group's lead was groundskeeper Luca Rossi, who had been with La Terre Felice for more than two decades. He maintained the property's lush gardens, vineyards, and olive groves, with the help of two dozen seasonal and full-time workers who he managed. Luca was middle-aged with weathered skin that spoke of years spent outdoors. His hands were calloused from labor, yet he moved with surprising grace.

His deep knowledge of the land and dedication to keeping it in pristine condition made him invaluable. His quiet, steady presence offered unwavering support to Gabby and Antoinette. As an old soul, his one true love was heeding the voice of Amelita Galli-Curci, the most famous Italian opera singer of the twentieth century.

Maria Russo, the housekeeper, was another long-time employee with a meticulous personality. She managed the guest rooms, ensuring every visitor felt at home. Maria had a close bond with Gabby, and she often stayed into the night to help with extra tasks to prepare for the next day's guest activities.

A nurturing, stout woman in her late fifties, Maria was almost like Gabby's second mother. She was always ready with a kind word or a hot *caffe* when Gabby was unwell. Maria had seen how minor ailments affected Gabby at an early age. They were more intense and took longer to resolve, yet everyone felt it was a simple nuance of living and working on a farm.

Paolo Bianchi owned the image of a strapping thirty-year-old farmhand. He proved himself dependable and hardworking by handling all the daily farm operations—from tending to the animals to assisting with the harvests.

For La Terre Felice, sheep and goats were part of the mix for their milk and cheese, along with cows, chickens, and other poultry. The estate was known for creating some of the best Pecorino Toscano in central Italy, a traditional cheese made from sheep's milk. Horses were also stabled and used for light farm work and guest riding.

Paolo committed to sustainable farming practices, and under his guidance, La Terre Felice implemented several environmentally friendly initiatives such as soil and water conservation, composting, rain harvesting, and wetland creation. His energy and innovative ideas kept the farm running as scheduled, so Gabby could focus on the broader issues of running a growing business. Despite Paolo's impressive work ethic, his approachable demeanor endeared him to both the staff and guests at La Terre Felice.

Travel concierge Sofia Marino was a ball of fire. A recent graduate of Università Bocconi in Milan, Sofia had recently joined the team to oversee all aspects of guest hospitality. Sofia made bookings, greeted guests, and ensured their stay exceeded memorable.

Sofia's warm, engaging personality and excellent organizational skills made her the perfect person to take on more guest-facing responsibilities, allowing Gabby to learn and understand more about agritourism. Sofia also took over marketing efforts, using social media to attract a younger and more targeted clientele to La Terre Felice.

Most important was Giuseppe Moretti, the chef's assistant. Mamma Antoinette's wingman collaborated with her in the kitchen, preparing meals and learning the secrets of traditional Italian cuisine. Giuseppe, who was called Pino, had grown up in a small village in Tuscany, surrounded by the rich flavors of Italian cooking. He had a deep respect for Antoinette and often took on more responsibilities of adjusting recipes and mixing and preparing the ingredients for guest meals.

Giuseppe's enthusiasm for cooking and his eagerness to learn from the best "mamma" ensured that the culinary experience at La Terre Felice always remained top-notch. He made sure the staff of three, who were handpicked because of their supportive talent and willingness to create traditional meals, enabled Pino to reap the benefit of being Antoinette's favorite. She was easy on the staff thanks to her wingman.

Chapter 8

Human Frailty and Strength

Over the years as Gabby matured, her health challenges began to affect the daily operations at La Terre Felice.

"I am determined to keep everything running smoothly," she had said to Maria, who like any nurturing "mother" was becoming increasingly concerned. "There are times when I will need to rely on our people, Maria, and I trust you will see when that is necessary."

Gabby's resilience in managing the *agriturismo* despite her health challenges inspired those around her. They served as a poignant reminder of human fragility and strength.

One recent day while Gabby attempted to carry too much wine to a scheduled event at La Terre Felice, she stumbled and shattered two cases of freshly chilled Vernaccia white wine. Pino was close by and witnessed the accident.

"Pino, please don't mention this to Antoinette," Gabby said. "I just stepped awkwardly on the cobblestone. It was a clumsy accident."

"Don't you worry, Gabby," Pino said. "We have more wine chilling. I'll get this cleaned up, quickly." Pino certainly knew of Gabby's health challenges, yet he saw her inner strength and determination to get beyond her limitations.

"Your mind and resilience are your real strengths, Gabby," he said. "We have your back, always."

Although Gabby's illness was always on her mind, it was less of a burden when she was active. The physical exertion necessary to run the agriturismo was taxing–lots of movement, lifting and energetic activity–but her determination pushed her beyond limitations.

"I cannot let this get me down," screamed her *inner voice. "Others cannot see me in times of distress. Fight, fight, fight."*

Between all of Gabby's responsibilities at the vineyard and mounting concerns about her health, she barely had a second to think about Gio. Having not had so much as a recent text from him, she'd pretty much stopped wondering if he would return or whether their relationship would survive.

But rather than dip her toe back into the dating pool for a fling, Gabby channeled every ounce of her energy into the business—sun up to sun down, sometimes forgetting to nourish herself during the day. It was her way of holding onto something stable when so much of her life was uncertain. Yet despite Gabby's intense focus, sometimes she let herself feel the weight of her circumstances. Late at night, after the guests were asleep and the property was peaceful except for the chirping crickets, she sat by the window in her room, gazing up at the stars.

I really miss him, Gabby thought. *We could be doing so much together if his nomadic life hadn't pulled him away again. I really miss his sexy charm, our talks, and making love.* Gabby struggled to push those thoughts out of her head, thinking, *There's no use dwelling on things I can't control.*

In four short months, Gabby's dedication had transformed La Terre Felice from a humble vineyard into a vogue *agriturismo.* News traveled fast, and it quickly became a popular destination for travelers searching for an authentic Tuscan experience.

One evening as the sun dipped below the horizon while guests were in conversation on the outdoor terrace, Gabby stood by in the corner. *It looks like an open Italian market,* she thought as she took in the mix of Australians, Asians, Scots, Brits, and of course, many Americans who would be occupying the estate's cottages that night.

Each night before Gabby's head hit the pillow, she peeked at the *agriturismo*'s reviews. Reading words like, "Tasty food and cozy accommodations" and "Filled with warmth and attentiveness" brought a glow to Gabby's heart. But her success felt hollow. Even though she was proud of all that she had achieved in a short time, it couldn't fill the hole left by Gio's absence.

Chapter 9

The Essence of Tradition

"**S**hake those trees!" Luca boomed one early September morning from the hill overlooking the groves, signaling the start of the fall olive harvest, a cherished tradition woven into the fabric of Italian culture. The crisp fall air was invigorating, filled with the promise of the season's bounty as the Rosetti family and their devoted staff along with four teams of ten workers assembled beneath the ancient olive trees, their branches laden with ripe fruit.

In Italy, the olive harvest begins with careful attention and precision. Large nets are placed beneath the heavy branches, poised to catch the precious olives as they fall. When ripened, the olives are deep purple, dark brown, and sometimes black. The darker the fruit, the richer the oil content. The workers shake with skilled hands and gentle yet firm motions, coaxing the olives to release their hold from the trees and tumble to the ground.

The rhythmic sound of swaying branches and falling olives creates a harmonious symphony that echoes throughout the grove. Each shake is a tribute to the generations that have nurtured and tended to the tree through seasons of growth and storms.

La Terre Felice guests were encouraged to work alongside the team and participate in seasonal activities, such as olive picking, grape harvesting, and cheese making. The *agriturismo* also sold extras for the locals at the weekly markets in the nearby village square, offering fresh produce, artisanal goods, and homemade preserves to villagers and tourists all prepared by the working staff.

This day in September, as the olives cascaded down, mother and daughter Rosetti and their loyal crew were reminded of the land's annual rebirth and the strength of the human spirit.

"It's our favorite time of the year, Mamma," Gabby said. "Like the olives, we weather daily challenges to ensure our ancestral soil provides nourishment. We draw stability from the earth and each other."

The sense of renewal, abundance, and hope from the harvest echoed feelings in Gabby's heart. For the past few weeks, her illness had been in remission. She felt better than she had in a very long time. Her mother took notice and was optimistic—however cautiously because she had seen ups and downs of Gabby's health for years.

After the trees have yielded their fruit over several day's work, Luca and Paolo carefully collected the nets and transferred the olives into woven baskets. A deep purple color glimmered in the sunlight, displaying the richness and bounty of the land.

Following the harvest, Luca drove the olives to the local mill, where they went through the traditional method of pressing and extracting to create the flavorful Felice olive oil.

This was part love and all tradition, embodying the timeless bond between the people of the villa and the land that sustained them. Under the Rosetti family's stewardship, some of the finest Tuscan olive oil had been produced.

Chapter 10

The Par for the Course

Always the vagabond, Gio had little communication with anyone during his travels, especially while taking winnings from other players on the golf course. Gabby hadn't heard from Gio much except for a few texts and a call or two over his time away. She was noticeably upset to everyone at La Terre Felice, yet Gabby kept that struggle to herself, refusing to reach out, knowing that Gio would eventually want to see her.

When Gio arrived after four months back at La Terre Felice, the warm, golden hues of the Tuscan countryside greeted him like an old friend. As he approached the estate, he felt an unfamiliar weight in his chest. The excitement of his travels, the articles he'd written, and the accolades he'd earned seemed hollow as he stepped back into the life he had left behind.

Gio also felt some trepidation, knowing he had neglected Gabby and their relationship while he had been away. *Will she welcome me with the same warmth? Or has my absence created a rift between us?* he wondered. The familiar scent of olive trees and lavender filled the air as Gio walked up the gravel path leading to the farmhouse. La Terre Felice was always beautiful, but Gio noticed something more—an unmistakable sense of vitality and growth. The once modest *agriturismo* was now alive with energy.

Gio saw guests mingling on the courtyard patio, enjoying wine and cheese under the shade of an olive canopy. He heard laughter dance through the air. He recognized Gabby's changes—every corner of the property had been well cared for and radiated refinement and magic.

As Gio got closer to the farmhouse, he spotted Gabby. She was standing near the vegetable garden, her hands dirty from picking fresh tomatoes off the vine. She looked radiant with a soft glow on her cheeks from the day's labor. But as Gio got closer, he saw a hardness in her eyes not seen before. It was as if the four months apart had fortified her resolve, and she had built up walls around herself.

When Gabby saw Gio approach, her body tensed for a moment before she wiped her hands on her apron and began to walk toward him. For a brief second, she felt a flicker of the old warmth between them, the shared history, the love that once felt unbreakable. But then, reality settled in.

"You're back," Gabby said, her voice steady but missing the affection that used to accompany their togetherness.

Gio hesitated, unsure of what to say. He searched her face for a sign, but Gabby as usual masked her emotions when necessary. "I'm back," he said with a hint of guilt in his voice. He thought, *I wish I could tell her how sorry I am. Being away for so long was never my intention. The stories I pursued were not worth the cost of losing her. But it's not that simple. Words may not be enough.*

Gabby nodded, looking away before turning back to him. "A lot has changed here since you've been gone. The *agriturismo* is doing great. Mamma and I … we've made it unique."

Gio saw the pride in her eyes, but he also sensed the underlying message: She didn't need him to make it happen. Seeing how she's thrived in his absence underscored that his leaving hurt her in ways he couldn't comprehend.

"I'm so proud of what you've done, Gabby," he said, his voice softer now. "La Terre Felice is amazing. You've made it into everything we dreamed of."

Gabby crossed her arms, her gaze steady. "I didn't do it for us, Gio. I did it because I had to. You were absent, and I couldn't wait, hoping you would return. I had to keep moving forward, for myself, for my family, for this place."

Gabby's words hit Gio like a punch in the gut. He wanted to argue, to tell her he must go, that he thought she understood his need to travel and to write. Deep down, he knew she was right. She had no choice but to continue without him.

"I'm sorry," Gio whispered, acknowledging the weight of his absence. "I should have been here. I should have—"

Gabby shook her head, cutting him off. "*No, Gio. Tu sei chi sei.* You needed to go, and I let you. I've changed. I couldn't live in limbo waiting for you to return."

A long, heavy silence fell between them. Gio could see how much stronger and more independent Gabby had become. She was not the same Gabby he left behind. She was still the woman he loved, still the heart of La Terre Felice, but now she was someone who learned to live without him. For a moment, the thought of losing Gabby for good paralyzed him. "What does that mean for us?" he asked, barely audibly.

Gabby's eyes softened, but there was a sadness in them. "I don't know, Gio. I've been trying to figure that out, but it's hard. I've spent the past four months focusing on this place because it was the only thing I could control. You're like the wind, impossible to hold onto."

Gio stepped closer to her, his heart pounding. "I don't want to lose you, Gabby. I love you. I always have."

She looked at him, and for a moment, she felt another flicker of the old love they shared. But it faded quickly, replaced by a weary understanding. "Love isn't enough anymore, Gio. I need stability. I must know that you won't disappear again when things get hard. Can you give me that?"

Gio hesitated. He wanted to say yes, to promise her the world, but he knew himself too well. The call of the open road and the stories waiting to be told had always pulled him away. Could he stay this time?

Before Gio could respond, Gabby put a hand on his arm. "You don't need to make a decision right now. Know this, Gio: La Terre Felice will always be here, and I will always care about you. But I can't just sit around here waiting for you to figure out what you want." Gabby turned and walked toward the farmhouse, leaving Gio behind.

A chill settled in. Gio realized that the life he thought he could return to might no longer exist.

Chapter 11

A Real Decision

"I'm upset with you, Gio. I believed we had something special," Gabby said the next morning during breakfast. "It's about respect, growing together, and not just saying you love me."

Gio felt the pang of her disappointment. "Bella, I do love and respect you. I want to be with you," he said. "That's why I'm asking you to let me stay and prove it to everyone."

After Gabby cautiously agreed to allow Gio to remain at the estate for a time—sleeping in the guest cottage—Gio spent the next several months working alongside Luca and Paolo. He sweated out the remains of the worldly stench he had exposed himself to for those recent assignments.

At first, Gabby had a difficult time accepting that Gio was back—and trusting that he wasn't going to run off again at a moment's notice. Gio showed uncharacteristic patience with her, working hard to regain her trust.

Under Gabby's discerning and piercing blue eyes, Gio gained her favor by working with Luca's team to redo a main guest terrace adjacent to one of the property's retention ponds. The work was tough, lifting heavy stones and gravel to create a stable pathway and viewing area of the sloped vineyard on the south side of the property. It turned into a stunning visual for the estate, especially when the sun dropped on the horizon in the evening.

"Gio, you've done a masterful job with that project," Gabby beamed. "And all I thought you could do was travel and write," she joked, finally bringing a bit of fun back into their conversation.

"I can do a lot, Gabby," Gio said. "My great-grandfather was a stone mason. It's in my blood."

"Let's celebrate and share a bottle of wine over dinner and continue our conversation," Gabby said, then thought, *Maybe Gio is back.*

Luca, Paolo, and the rest of the staff knew that Gio planned to propose to Gabby, yet they respected his wishes of complete silence.

"Don't worry, Giovanni, your secret is safe with Paolo and me," Luca said. "And to prove it, we'll share some of our homemade grappa after lunch."

Over this visit, Gio grew closer to Gabby's mother, too. He respected Antoinette as the older female head of the household, and of course, he loved her cooking, especially the manicotti. In Mamma, he glimpsed the mature beauty he imagined Gabby would age into.

Mamma, on the other hand, took longer to warm up to Gio. He broke her daughter's heart once; she wasn't eager to let him have a second go of it. But she quietly watched Gio work with Luca and Paolo, observing him hone his skills. She was impressed by Gio's work ethic. She had to admit Gio seemed happy at the estate, and he looked at Gabby with such love in his eyes.

Gio often joined Antoinette for lunch in the farmhouse dining room. One afternoon after a delicious lunch of roasted eggplant, sun-dried tomatoes with penne pasta, and a nice burrata salad, all washed down with a medium-bodied Chianti, Gio blurted, "Antoinette, I want to marry Gabriella."

"Are you asking for my permission, young man?" she asked. "Or are you telling me?"

"*Le mi scusi*, Antoinette. Of course, with your blessing and with all respect."

"You have my permission, Gio, if she'll have you," Antoinette said nodding.

With Antoinette's blessing secured, Gio searched the property for the next many days for the right location to propose to Gabby. At night, he held her in his arms, sitting and watching the flames of the courtyard fire pits before carrying her to bed.

Gio decided to propose to Gabby in a quiet grove amongst the olive trees on a hill overlooking the resplendence of La Terre Felice. With its serene beauty and deep connection to the land and their shared history, this place felt like the right spot to ask her to share a life with him. The pair had shared many quiet moments there, talking about their dreams and the future of La Terre Felice.

Gio spent the next few days carefully planning the proposal. He wanted everything to be perfect—to reflect his love and respect for Gabby and the life they were building together.

On the evening of the proposal, Gio led Gabby up the hill, her hand in his. The path was familiar, but tonight, it felt different, charged with the significance of what was about to happen. As they reached the grove with the sun beginning its colorful set, the air filled with the earthy scent of olive trees, and the gentle rustling of the leaves added to the tranquil atmosphere.

Gio set up a small picnic in the grove—a bottle of their best wine, fresh bread, and some of Antoinette's homemade cheese. Gabby smiled when she saw the display, touched by the thoughtfulness of the gesture. They sat together, enjoying the moment, talking and laughing as they had often done.

Gio felt his heart race. It was time. He took Gabby's hand and looked into her eyes, filled with love and curiosity. "Gabby," he began, his voice soft but steady. "This place, La Terre Felice, is where I found my true self. It's where I truly found you. Everything you've built here, everything that we've shared, is more than I ever could have dreamed of. I've traveled the world, but nowhere has ever felt like home until being with you."

Gabby's eyes widened slightly, her breath catching as she realized what was happening. Gio reached into his pocket and pulled out a small velvet box. Opening it, he revealed a simple yet elegant ring—a perfect symbol of their love, crafted by a local jeweler who understood that as the Tuscan land sustains and nurtures, so the ring must signify a promise to grow together, too.

"Gabby, you are my home. You are why this place is so unique, and I want to spend the rest of my life with you here. Will you marry me?"

Tears welled up in Gabby's eyes, and she nodded, unable to speak. She squeezed his hand tightly, then whispered, "Yes, Gio. Of course, yes."

Gio slipped the ring onto her finger, his heart swelling with joy and relief. They embraced, holding each other close as the sun set, leaving them bathed in the twilight of the Tuscan evening in a moment of pure happiness, a promise of a future filled with love, laughter, and the land that had brought them together. Gabby leaned her head on Gio's shoulder as stars began to appear in the night sky, heralding the beginning of a new chapter in their lives—one that they would write in tandem in the place that had become their shared dream.

Chapter 12

The Wedding

As Gio and Gabby planned their wedding and honeymoon, their relationship continued to be marked by unpredictability. They navigated their differences; however, Gio's restless spirit often clashed with Gabby's desire for stability.

Despite these challenges, their love blossomed. Having felt they had spent significant time together, they decided to leap into marriage. This decision brought them joy, but it also brought subtle anxiety for Gio, who found it arduous to imagine settling down.

They envisioned a spring wedding, a lovely, intimate gathering at La Terre Felice in the courtyard beside the sloped vineyard that had come to symbolize their shared journey. Gabby poured her heart into the wedding preparations, aiming to make the day a true reflection of their love and the life they had built together.

The vineyard was starting to bloom, with rows of vibrant and green grapevines, and the air filled with the delightful scents of roses and lavender that Gabby had planted for the occasion.

Friends and family were eager to come together to celebrate the union of two people who seemed destined for each other.

The heart of the nearby village pulsed with life, too, where the streets and alleyways converged into a busy piazza. Daily, the air filled with baked bread from bakeries, while the rich scent of espresso poured out of the cafes. Laughter and animated conversations resonated everywhere as villagers gathered for their daily *passeggiata*, creating a symphony of voices that blended with the distant tolling of church bells.

The brilliant colors of the markets with their ripened produce and handmade crafts added to the town's excitement. After all, a celebration was on tap, painting the final touches on a most picturesque scene for all to enjoy.

As the wedding day approached, Gio became consumed with doubt. The thought of committing himself to one place and one life for eternity felt like a heavy weight on his shoulders. He loved Gabby, but the idea of being tied down terrified him. On the wedding morning, Gio woke early, his mind racing. He wandered through the vineyard, the place that had become both a home and a source of anxiety for him.

As he walked among the vines, he thought about the life he and Gabby had talked about—running the *agriturismo* together, building a future at La Terre Felice, staying in one place.

It was a beautiful vision, but not the life he had ever imagined.

As the hours ticked by, Gio's anxiety grew. He returned to the small cottage where he resided, trying to calm himself down, but the fear wouldn't subside.

He loved Gabby more than anything, but he couldn't shake the fact that he was about to make a mistake—a decision that would trap him and hurt the person he cared about most.

Gabby was in her room getting ready for the ceremony. She was nervous but excited to start this new chapter in their lives. She had sensed Gio's unease in the days leading up to the big event but convinced herself it was only pre-wedding jitters. After all, they worked through so much together. She was sure they could also get through this.

As the guests began to arrive and the ceremony approached, Gio disappeared. Gabby, dressed in her white gown, waited in the small room near the courtyard, expecting him to appear at any moment. As the minutes passed, her excitement turned to worry.

Franco Reno, Gio's best friend and best man, who met Gabby early in her relationship with Gio, went searching. Over the past months, Franco and Gabby had become close, too, bonding over a shared sense of style in life, a love of art, and a strong, disciplined work ethic.

Franco was born in Viterbo, and he maintained a home in the village located north of Rome. He also leased accommodations nearby at Toscana Resort Castelfalfi in the heart of Tuscany, where he continued to hone his skills as a professional golfer and a standout on the DP World Tour. He was dedicated to his craft and ready to take Gio's money on any course.

As soon as Franco reached Gio's cottage, he realized something was wrong. He found the cottage empty along with a written apology, brimming with regret and confusion. Gio had vanished, unable to go through with the wedding, leaving his best friend uncertain about when or if he would return. Franco read the words with great trepidation.

My Bella Gabriella,

Words cannot begin to describe what my actions have done to you, Antoinette, and everyone at La Terre Felice today. I am truly sorry, but I am so confused. I love you more than anything, yet my spirit feels caged, and I have to leave. I know I have hurt you so much. I hope in time you will understand.

Ciao, Amore Mio, Gio

Driven by his friend's choice, Franco realized he had to tell Gabby. He approached her with a heavy heart, searching for the right words.

"Gabby, Gio's gone. He left La Terre Felice—" Franco said.

Hearing the news that a part of her feared would happen, Gabby's world crumbled. The man she loved, the one she prepared to spend her life with, left her at the altar. She was devastated, humiliated, and bewildered. She couldn't understand how Gio could have done something so cruel.

Franco informed the guests that the wedding was off. Many lingered, offering their condolences, but Gabby was inconsolable.

Antoinette was irate. She was willing to walk alongside her daughter and give her over to this writer, but now, in proper Italian form, she just wanted to hit him over the head with a rolling pin.

In the following days, Gabby struggled to understand what had happened. She recognized Gio as a free spirit, but she had believed their love was strong enough to face his fears. A sense of betrayal came from Gio's absence and the painful realization that he had not been honest with her—or maybe even with his doubts.

Gio was filled with guilt and remorse. He left La Terre Felice because he couldn't bear the thought of making Gabby miserable. He convinced himself it was better to leave her than resent her for his chosen life later. Even as he fled, he understood he was leaving behind the best thing that ever happened to him.

The aftermath of Gio's departure devastated both. Heartbroken and humiliated, Gabby threw herself back into work at La Terre Felice, trying to keep the pieces of her life together. Gio wandered through his comforting haunts in Italy and Spain to clear his head, unsure of what to do, conflicted by the thought of the life he just walked away from.

Though separated by miles and the weight of Gio's betrayal, their love still lingered but was now tainted by pain. Both lives would never be the same, and they were left to pick up the pieces in their own ways.

Chapter 13

The Chronic Illness's Return

In the days and weeks that followed Gio's betrayal, Gabby felt like a shadow of her former self. Perhaps it was the profound stress and crushing depression that brought on the sudden return of her illness, which intensified the hurt of being left at the altar.

The autoimmune disease that affected her for years flared up as if her body reacted to the emotional upheaval. Her health took a rapid downturn, and before long, she was rushed to the hospital, her condition worsening.

Gabby's autoimmune disease had started in her early thirties, coinciding with her increased responsibilities at La Terre Felice after her father's death. At first, the symptoms were mild—fatigue, joint pain, and occasional fever—which she attributed to the stress and physical demands of running the *agriturismo*. However, the symptoms became more persistent and challenging as time passed.

Gabby's doctors recommended bio-regenerative therapy (BRT), a treatment designed to manage and reverse the effects of her chronic autoimmune disease. BRT involves harvesting a patient's stem cells, then modifying and reintroducing them into the body to help repair the immune system.

Each patient was unique and responded differently, yet this new modality had the potential to transform care for Gabby. Otherwise, a steady diet of immunosuppressive drugs and steroids remained the protocol, making each remission and recovery more challenging.

Gio and Gabby's friend Franco checked in on Gabby frequently, monitoring her physical and mental health. He was surprised and saddened to see both failing so badly.

"Would you consider reaching out to Gio?" he asked. "Or I could on your behalf. I know that he would want to know how you are doing."

Gabby trusted Franco and considered his suggestion, but only for a brief moment. She was determined not to let Gio know. She couldn't stand the idea of him returning out of guilt or obligation. She would only have wanted him to return if he wanted to, not because he felt he had to. She made Franco swear not to tell Gio about her condition.

"Promise me, Franco," she said, her voice weak but stubborn as she lay in the hospital bed. "He can't know. If he finds out, it should be because he chose to return on his own, not because you informed him."

Franco paused, caught between his loyalty to Gio and his worry for Gabby's health. However, seeing the resolve in her eyes, he consented. "I promise, Gabby. But if he asks, I won't lie to him."

Gabby nodded, grateful for Franco's understanding. If Gio returned, it would be because he had found the strength to confront his fears and commit to their planned life. Until then, she would fight the illness on her own, with the support of Franco, Antoinette, and the others at La Terre Felice.

During the next few weeks, Franco was everything Gio was unable to be—diligent, organized, and most of all available as the conduit for Antoinette and the *agriturismo*. Other people saw how well Franco carried himself and his consistent approach to solving problems while communicating with Gabby's doctors and caregivers. Another skill of Franco's was always being there to clean up Gio's messes.

Franco visited Gabby at the hospital daily until his pro golfing career required him to travel to Scotland for an upcoming tour event. He always shared news from La Terre Felice and did his best to keep Gabby's spirits up. But no matter how hard Franco tried, the void left by Gio turned into a pain that no effort could mend.

As the days spent in the hospital dragged on, everyone was exhausted and filled with doubt. A hospital-acquired infection had taken hold in

Gabby's body. Still, she was strong-willed with a warrior personality. She cursed her adversary, and her spirit would not be broken, even when she confronted daunting health challenges.

Chapter 14

Resilience and Renaissance

Under the careful watch of her doctors and support from Antoinette, Gabby slowly began to regain her strength. Each day, she fought back with physical and mental focus, fueled by the desire to return to La Terre Felice.

Gabby's journey was demanding, but her unwavering determination made the difference. After several weeks of treatment, her condition improved. The doctors were amazed by her strength and her body's remarkable ability to keep battling.

More than medical treatment brought Gabby back. Her love for La Terre Felice, the life she built there, and the people who had become her family were all part of the recovery process.

The day that Gabby was finally strong enough to be released from the hospital, Antoinette and Luca arrived to take her home. The drive back was filled with emotion, gratitude, and relief. As they approached the familiar landscape and saw the farmhouse on the hill, Gabby felt a rush of emotion. This was where she belonged, the place that fit her best.

Upon arriving, she was welcomed with tears of joy by the staff and workers who had missed her so much. They kept the *agriturismo* running in her absence, but it was not quite the same without her.

A profound sense of peace washed over Gabby as she stepped out of the car and onto the ground. The air was fresh, the sun warmed her face, and the land embraced her return. She wandered through the vineyards, olive groves, and gardens, taking every sight, scent, and sound. This was her life, her legacy, and she was ready to embrace it once more.

At night, Gabby retreated into a quiet sanctuary adjacent to her room at La Terre Felice. It provided easy access to her daily treatments and necessary consultations—and a place to indulge in her artwork. The room overlooked the vineyard, too, offering serene views and triggering a calmness that contributed to Gabby's internal well-being.

With Gabby's health restored and her spirit renewed, she returned to work with a fresh purpose. She threw herself into the day-to-day operations of La Terre Felice, overseeing every detail with the same passion and dedication that defined her. Inspired by her recovery, the workers rallied around her.

Gabby also brought a sense of healing to those around her. Franco, who had carried the weight of her illness and Gio's secret, saw the light return to her eyes.

Antoinette had prayed to Santa Caterina di Siena every day for her daughter's recovery, and she was filled with gratitude and love for St. Catherine's answer. Together, everyone worked La Terre Felice to its glory, and in doing so, they restored normalcy and hope to their lives.

"I know this illness could return," Gabby said to Antoinette. "But for now, I am alive. I am home, and that's what matters most."

Gio's absence still lingered in Gabby's heart, but she focused on the present, on the life she was given another chance to continue. La Terre Felice was everything, and as long as she had it, she could face whatever the future held.

La Terre Felice was a success, and that was enough. The *agriturismo* served as a destination for travelers eager to experience Tuscany's charm and as a refuge for artists and wanderers from around the globe. It welcomed writers, painters, sculptors, and musicians, offering them the inspiration of the rolling hills and the peacefulness of the Tuscan lifestyle.

Gabby was more than just the co-owner; she was an artist renowned for her paintings, embodying the Italian countryside's spirit. From a young age, she dedicated herself to the arts and studied in Florence, where the rich culture and history of the region infused her creativity.

Her brown hair had grown darker over the years, and her eyes still shone with a brilliance that could pierce even the coldest of hearts. She was living her dream and dealing with health issues, but beneath the surface of her beauty and accomplished life lay one significant imperfection—her profound, unreciprocated love for the wandering Gio.

Chapter 15

A Late-Night Knock

One lovely autumn evening, Gabby and her mother enjoyed wine from their vineyard on the terrace. The air was rich with the aroma of ripening grapes and the distant sound of cicadas.

Antoinette, a committed supporter of organic farming, relished her wine. "Gabby, can you believe how far we've come from that rundown farmhouse to this thriving villa?"

Gabby smiled. "It's been a wonderful journey. I remember when we first arrived; it was a bit hectic, but I could sense its potential. And now look at it—a piece of paradise."

Antoinette chuckled as she reflected on their initial challenges. "The vineyards were in complete disarray when Antonio and I acquired the property, and the olive groves needed lots of care," she remarked. "We got to work, rolled up our sleeves. Little by little, we brought everything back to flourish."

Gabby raised her glass. "To hard work, perseverance, and family."

"To realize our dreams," Antoinette said, clinking her glass with Gabby's.

La Terra Felice earned a reputation for its commitment to sustainability and the farm-to-table philosophy. The estate produced award-winning wines and olive oil, complemented by a thriving organic garden that supplied fresh produce.

Antoinette leaned back in her chair, a content smile on her face. "Do you remember when people questioned our choice of organic farming? Now, that's what makes us stand out."

Gabby nodded, recalling the skeptics who doubted their venture's viability.

"We committed to our vision," Gabby noted. "We aimed to create a place where people could connect with nature, enjoy exquisite food, and experience the charm of Tuscany."

They reminisced about the guests who had become like family and often returned year after year. People from all over the world visited La Terra Felice to escape the fast pace of city life for the peace in the calm and beauty of the countryside.

"I love that our guests leave with more than just memories," Gabby remarked. "They depart with a deeper appreciation for the land, the food, and the Italian community we've nurtured."

Antoinette agreed. "They might come for a vacation, but they're also learning about sustainable living and supporting local farmers. It's a complete experience."

As night fell, mother and daughter continued to share stories, laughter, and dreams for the future of La Terra Felice. Their *agriturismo* was thriving and became a source of inspiration for people longing for a genuine connection to the good life—*la dolce vita.*

Just when Gabby and Antoinette were about to call it an evening, they heard a Vespa approaching up the hill of the estate. Little did they know how the knock on the door that would follow would send everyone's life into another dimension.

Chapter 16

Franco and the Travel Writer

Among the few constants in Gio's life was his best friend, Franco. The pair had met as young, aspiring dreamers several years ago outside Rome—where else but at a golf tournament. Gio was hustling and covering the Italian Open where Franco was a strapping young golfer new to tour events. Gio interviewed Franco over drinks after the final round where they instantly connected and developed a strong and lasting friendship.

Unlike Gio, Franco was the epitome of stability. A professional golfer, he had earned a reputation for his unwavering focus and commitment to the sport.

Franco had many friends among the players on tour and a strong business network of outside interests. He was a towering figure of stability and the antithesis of Gio's free-spirited, nomadic existence.

Single and tall with broad shoulders tapered to a slim waist, Franco's presence on the golf course was marked by quiet confidence. His movements were deliberate, and each swing of the club was a testament to years of disciplined practice. Off the green, Franco favored classic Italian suits, contrasting Gio's more casual, adventurous wardrobe.

While Gio chased dreams across the globe, Franco found solace in the traditions and routines of a professional lifestyle. His calm, collected demeanor hinted at a man who valued discipline. Yet, beneath the polished exterior, warmth and loyalty defined his friendship with Gio.

Franco often played the role of Gio's anchor, a steadying force attempting to bring order to the chaos that seemed to follow his friend. He was a pragmatic counterbalance to Gio's spontaneous nature. In their friendship, they found harmony, each providing what the other lacked or perhaps desired.

Despite their contrasting personalities, Gio and Franco's connection was built on the links and deepened by life's difficulties. Franco was reliable when Gio's escapades veered off course, providing direction and a gentle reminder of what mattered most.

One recent day, Franco called Gio as the wanderlust stood amidst the lush greens of a posh new resort just outside Barcelona.

"Gio," Franco's calm and measured voice said. "I've heard you want to reconnect with Gabby. Is that true?"

Gio sighed a hint of nostalgia, saying, "Yeah, *paisan*. It's time."

"Well, you better do it right this time, *mio amico*," Franco replied. "Italy is a land of deep connections, passion, and *familia*. Gabby still has the scars from what you did."

Gio's heart skipped a beat. Gabby was always on his mind. "I know, Franco. I've got to make amends."

"You left her alone at the altar, *stunod*," reminded his friend. "In front of her family and friends and most of the village. That would certainly put a bounty on your head."

"Fucked that one up, for sure," Gio said. "I was a mess, out of control. I had to escape."

"There's a saying in life, my friend," chimed Franco. "It says that out of conflict and the sewers of despair, a person can rise carrying a gold watch. For every bad, comes some good." That was Gio Marzo.

Chapter 17

The Profound Wanderer's Knock

Lost and away for many months, Gio found his way back to La Terra Felice. His journey back to Gabby's home in the Tuscan countryside would be a welcome chance to rest and recover from the emotional whirlwind of many months of working and despair.

When Gabby saw him standing on the farmhouse porch, hand poised to knock, she felt a rush of emotion that almost dropped her to the floor. "Gio! What are you doing here?"

"I had to see you. I need to explain," he said.

With the quickness of a siren cat, Gabby put fingers to Gio's lip to keep him from uttering a word.

"You left me cold, Gio. Am I now supposed to accept you with warmth and open arms?" Gabby scolded. "That day would have been magical, the night full of passionate lovemaking. All you did was fuck me and everyone here in the worst way."

"Gabby, I … I …"

"Shut up, Gio," she said. "You're lucky Antoinette is waiting until tomorrow to talk to you. She wanted to kill you for that stunt you pulled."

As they continued to talk between terse moments, Gio declared that he had fulfilled his obligations. "Now I truly am ready to settle down so that we can be together," Gio said urgently.

Gabby was hesitant, reminding him about the times he had deserted her. "You've made that clear on many occasions, but how could I ever trust you when you keep leaving," she said.

Gabby was still angry at Gio, and now she was also furious at herself at how the iciness in her heart was melting already. Her nature lacked any bitterness, especially toward this man who dripped with charisma and always captivated her with his rugged charm.

"I've accepted one final travel writing assignment before I would like to settle down here for good—if you'll have me," Gio suggested. "I need to go to Rome in late September for the upcoming Ryder Cup. This is the biannual match between top golfers from the United States against the best of Europe, and hopefully I'll get to write about Franco and a remarkable victory for the Europeans against a formidable American team. I desperately wanted to see you and try to make amends before I go. And then after the Cup, I'll be here with you for good."

"Do you remember the last time you said that to me?" Gabby asked. "But our wedding altar was cold, and my heart emptied that day."

Gio looked at Gabby and stood. For once words escaped him and he gave a wry smile, turned, and left the room. Gabby held fast knowing that their issues still needed to be resolved. It would have to wait for now.

"Gio, sleep on the couch until you leave for Rome," she said.

Chapter 18

Fairways, Festivities, and Follies

After leaving the farmhouse, Gio drove the 200 kilometers to Rome, venting some of his frustration by taking some curves faster than most would deem safe. He checked into his hotel, located in the historic center of the city's classy Monti neighborhood.

As Gio exited his hotel, the warm Roman sun wrapped him as he headed to the golf course. With its blend of ancient charm and vibrant energy, Rome provided the ideal setting for the 2023 Ryder Cup, and Gio was excited to be part of the coverage.

The city embraced the golfing world at Marco Simone Golf and Country Club. Blending its rich history with the excitement of the tournament that had rotated every two years between America and Europe, this was the first time the cup would be contested on Italian soil. Italy, with all its beauty, had about as many golf courses in the entire country as the city of Los Angeles in California. So it was something special for all Italians to now be on the world stage.

For Gio, it was more than golf. With its captivating fusion of history, culture, and enjoyment, Rome had a way of embedding itself into your soul. He had attended many Ryder Cup tournaments, but this one felt unique. Rome made everything feel more vibrant, more alive, and Gio was eager to soak it all in.

He could sense the city's heartbeat as he strolled through the narrow, cobblestone streets. The buzz of scooters, the scent of brewed espresso, and the distant chime of church bells all contributed to the ambiance. Rome had its distinct rhythm, and Gio was in tune with it.

He took his time making his way to the course, taking a detour through a quiet *piazza* where a group of older men were playing bocce. He paused to watch, fascinated by their skill and how they laughed and argued in rapid Italian. He caught the eye of a local, who offered him a small glass of limoncello. Gio accepted with a grin, raising his glass in a silent toast before downing the shot. The sweet, sharp lemon hit awakened him even more.

As Gio arrived at the course, the first day of matches was about to tee off, and the excitement in the air was palpable. The difference between the historic city and the immaculate, contemporary fairways was remarkable. The course was a marvel of design, a green oasis nestled just outside the historic city. Gio felt a rush of excitement—both from the tournament and the lingering warmth of the limoncello.

He went to the media center, where the usual chaos of journalists typing on laptops, conducting interviews, and sharing predictions was in full swing. Gio found a seat by the window to see the first tee. He loved this part of his job—the thrill of live sports, the unpredictability of each match, and the challenge of capturing it all in words.

Of course Gio would follow Franco, a rising star on the European team, throughout the tournament. Franco's style was his calm demeanor on the course and a flair for drama—a dangerous combination in match play. He could turn a match around with a single swing, and Gio was eager to see how he would perform on his home soil.

As the day unfolded, he followed Franco's play. The Italian was in top form, driving the ball into fairways, hitting greens, and sinking putts. The crowd loved him, chanting his name and waving the Italian *Tricolour* whenever he approached a green.

Gio could see why Franco had become such a fan favorite. His manner was magnetic, a blend of confidence and charm that was uniquely Italian. He managed to grab a quick interview with Franco after his round. The golfer, still buzzing from his four-ball victory, was all smiles.

"Playing in Rome, in front of these fans, is a dream," Franco said, his voice full of pride. "This city, this course—it brings out the best in me."

Gio could see the gleam in Franco's eye, the fire that had driven his twosome to victory. This tournament meant more to him than most, and Gio had a great story on his hands. As Gio typed up his notes, his mind wandered back to the city beyond the course. The matches were intense, but so was his desire to explore more of Rome.

When the final putt of the day dropped, and the crowd erupted in cheers, Gio experienced that familiar rush of satisfaction that comes from a day well spent. But as the sun dipped, his thoughts shifted to the night ahead.

Later that evening, after filing his story, Gio meandered through the winding streets of Trastevere near Piazza Trilussa. The neighborhood buzzed with life—street musicians playing lively melodies, couples strolling hand in hand, and the mouthwatering aroma of food drifting from trattorias.

Gio was drawn to a small bar in an alley, the sounds of laughter and clinking glasses spilling out onto the street. Inside, the atmosphere was electric, a blend of locals and tourists all caught up in the evening's joy. He ordered a Negroni, the bartender serving it with a flourish, and settled into a corner booth to soak it all in.

The night took on a life of its own. Gio found himself chatting with a group of Italians who insisted on buying him drinks, their animated stories and laughter filling the space around them. A woman with dark, sparkling eyes caught his attention, and soon, they were sharing a bottle of wine at a table in the corner, the rest of the bar fading into the background while she playfully worked her hand down inside the front of his trousers.

Rome at night had a way of awakening the senses, making everything possible. The conversation flowed, a mix of broken English and Italian, the words becoming less important than the connection they shared. Gio knew he should be back at the hotel, resting for the next day's coverage, but the city had other plans for him.

As the night wore on, Gio and his new friends wandered through the streets, illuminated by the soft glow of streetlights. They found themselves by the Tiber, the river reflecting the city's lights, a bottle of Prosecco passed around as they sat on the steps, discussing life, love, sport, and everything in between.

When Gio returned to his hotel, it was well past midnight. The streets were quieter now, and the city was settling into its slumber. He was experiencing a heady mix of exhaustion and exhilaration, which only comes from a night of indulgence in a place like Rome.

Chapter 19

Midnight in Rome

The next day, Gio woke with a slight headache but a smile on his face—the previous night's memories blended with the excitement of another day at the Ryder Cup. Rome had its way of merging work and pleasure into one seamless experience. As Gio got ready to cover the tournament, he was again part of something extraordinary.

Leaning back in his chair, Gio's eyes roamed the busy media center while he wrapped up his latest article. The morning was a flurry of match updates, player interviews, and the constant buzz surrounding the Ryder Cup. Now that he was finished for the day, the Roman night beckoned him again.

Stepping outside into the cool evening air, he sensed the vibrant energy at the hotel. Rome had a knack for making every night an adventure waiting to unfold. He decided to go to Piazza Navona, one of his favorite places in the city. With its stunning baroque fountains and lively cafés, the piazza was always festive with activity.

Wandering through the square, Gio noticed a street performer—an older gentleman playing the accordion. His melody contrasted with the lively conversations around him. Gio dropped a few euros into the man's hat, pausing to let the music surround him.

The simplicity of the moment resonated within Gio. He was in one of the world's most electric cities, surrounded by a rich tapestry of history, passion, and an almost surreal sense of timelessness.

The streets of Rome guided him like an old friend as he continued walking. Gio found himself in a small wine bar, its dim lighting and comfortable atmosphere a perfect escape from outside noise. The bar was tucked away in the corner of Campo de Fiori, a square branded for its lively market during the day and cozy nightlife after dark.

He ordered a glass of Barolo and settled into a corner, watching as the bar slowly filled with locals and a few tourists who had stumbled upon this hidden gem. The night was still young, and the conversation around him blended laughter, flirtation, and the easy camaraderie that seemed to come naturally in Rome.

Just as Gio began to relax, he heard a familiar voice call his name. He looked up to see Franco striding towards him with a grin.

Still dressed in his team colors, the pro golfer looked like he had just stepped off the course. His presence drew a few curious glances from other patrons, but he seemed unfazed as if blending his professional life with the city's nightlife was second nature.

"Gio! I thought I might find you somewhere like this," Franco said, clapping his friend on the shoulder before sliding into the seat across from him. "You look like you've had a good day."

The writer laughed, lifting his glass in a mock toast. "Covering the Ryder Cup in Rome? How could I not? What about you? Shouldn't you be resting for tomorrow's matches?"

Franco waved off the concern with a casual flick of his wrist. "I'll be fine. Besides, tonight is too beautiful to waste on sleep. And I could use a drink after today's round." He signaled the bartender, who brought over another glass and poured Franco a generous helping of wine. As the friends clinked glasses, Gio could see the fatigue in Franco's eyes.

The pressure of playing in front of a home crowd, in a tournament as prestigious as the Ryder Cup, and for no money was no small thing. But there was also a spark there—a determination that Gio had seen on the course earlier.

They talked about the day's matches. Franco recounted an agitated moment on the sixteenth hole where he sunk a crucial birdie putt. The conversation flowed easily, transitioning from golf to stories of their experiences in Rome. Franco, it turned out, was as much a lover of the

Lazio region as his friend, and the two shared a mutual appreciation for its hidden corners and late-night adventures.

As the night wore on, Franco suggested they take a walk, and Gio agreed, eager to see where the night would lead. The two men wandered through the winding streets, the conversation shifting to more personal topics—life on tour, the sacrifices made for success, and the fleeting nature of such moments.

They ended up on a terrace overlooking the city, and the lights of Rome spread out before them. Franco leaned on the railing, his gaze distant. "Sometimes I wonder what it's all for. The fame, the pressure—it can be overwhelming. But nights like this, and it's all worth it," he said.

Gio nodded, understanding completely. "Rome has a way of putting things in perspective. It's a city that shows you're alive and reminds you that life is more than just the next win."

Franco smiled a genuine, tired smile that spoke of both contentment and the weight of expectation. "Maybe that's why I love it here so much. It's a place where you can forget—if only briefly."

They stood in companionable silence, the city humming quietly below them. Eventually, they returned to the bar where they started the evening.

Franco bid Gio, "*Buonanotte*. Don't miss my tee time tomorrow."

Gio laughed at the joke, shaking Franco's hand before watching him leave.

The evening had taken on a reflective tone, and as Gio returned to his hotel, he couldn't help but think about his connection with his longtime friend. In a city as vast and eternal as Rome, it was easy to feel small. Yet moments like this reminded Gio of the shared humanity that linked them together—athlete and writer, local and visitor, dreamer and realist.

Rome drew out these connections, making the extraordinary accessible and the mundane magical. Gio would carry these memories with him for as long as he lived—experiences woven together by the city's ancient streets and vibrant spirit.

And as the Ryder Cup continued to unfold, Gio was sure of one thing: Rome, with all its beauty, chaos, and wonder, was as much a part of the tournament as the matches themselves. And for that, he was grateful.

Chapter 20

The Heat of the Night

Gio woke the following day in the middle of a torrential rainstorm. Through the curtains of his hotel room, he saw a reminder that Rome weather didn't pause for anyone, not even a slightly hungover travel writer.

The memories of the previous night lingered: Franco's candid reflections, the city lights, and the quiet moments of understanding that had passed between them. It was rare to connect with someone on that level, especially in the fast-paced world of professional sports.

As the day unfolded, Gio pushed those thoughts aside, focusing instead on getting to Marco Simone for the matches. The Ryder Cup was heating up, and the singles match was waiting to unfold toward the finale. Franco was in top form, and Gio felt his excitement build. The anticipation was like a charged current.

Unfortunately, the rain was relentless that day, leaving the course unplayable and the golf postponed. The day was a washout. Time passed in a blur of updates, interviews, and hurried notes. Gio was ready to unwind. Returning to the media center, a different kind of anticipation began to take hold. Rome embraced him so far, offering generous doses of pleasure, and tonight, he would be indulging in whatever the city had left to offer.

As Gio wrapped up his work and prepared to leave, he thought about the lively crowds that had filled the course earlier in the day, particularly the women, their bright rain outfits and infectious energy adding a vibrant pulse to the tournament.

One woman had caught his eye. Petite, with flowing dark hair and an air of confidence, she stood out in the crowd of spectators. She was dressed in a sleek outfit that perfectly balanced elegance with the casual flair of a golf fan who gained attention. Her laugh was infectious, her tight features dazzling, and Gio found his eyes drifting back to her more than once.

As it turned out, just as Gio was about to leave the media center, he saw her again. She was leaning against a wall, chatting with a friend, a glass of Prosecco in her hand.

When she noticed Gio, her smile grew more expansive, and she excused herself from the conversation, approaching him with the poise of someone confident in her ability to get exactly what she wanted.

"You're Gio Marzo, right? The writer?" she asked, her voice as smooth as the wine she sipped.

Gio blinked, surprised. "That's right. And you are—?"

"Valentina," she replied, offering her hand with a teasing look. "I've seen you around the course these past few days. Figured it was about time we met."

Gio shook her hand, and the warmth of her touch lingered. "Nice to meet you, Valentina. You've got a keen eye to have spotted me in that crowd."

She laughed a musical sound that sent a thrill through him. "I've always had a thing for words. And for the people who know how to use them."

Gio chuckled, the flirtation crackled between them like static electricity to his groin. "Well, if you like words, maybe I can buy you a drink and talk about them."

Valentina's eyes sparkled with mischief. "I would like that. Let's skip the bar. I know a place with a better view."

Before Gio could reply, Valentina slipped her arm through his and led him into a taxi back to the city and down a side street, away from the noise of the main drag. They stepped outside and strolled through the winding alleys, the city's lively energy surrounding them. It didn't take long to find a hidden rooftop terrace at Palazzo Galla, perched high above with stunning views of the illuminated Colosseum and skyline.

The rain from earlier had subsided, leaving the city in a warm, golden light, with the domes and spires of Rome stretching out in the distance. The bar was inviting, with a few tables scattered about and soft music playing in the background. It was the kind of place where secrets could be whispered and desires explored.

They settled at a table near the edge, the view taking Gio's breath away. Valentina indeed held his attention. As they talked, she leaned in closer, her laughter sending delightful shivers down his spine. She was witty, charming, and bold, her hand brushing against his arm or leg, sending electric jolts.

Gio was getting lost in that moment. The wine flowed, and their conversation grew more personal and intimate. Valentina shared her passion for the game, the thrill she experienced while watching the matches, and the excitement of being so close to the action. Gio recounted stories covering the tour, tales of late nights, close calls, and the bond between players and fans.

The sexual tension between them became almost unbearable. Valentina's eyes never left his, her intentions clear. After a charged silence, she leaned in and kissed him, her lips soft and inviting. Gio responded, his hand finding the small of her back as he pulled her closer.

The kiss began a night that would leave them breathless. They left the bar, the city's lights guiding them through the streets back to Gio's hotel. The following hours were a blur of animal passion and indulgence, the night Rome seemed to specialize in.

In the dim light of his hotel room, Gio and Valentina explored each other with the urgency of two people who only wanted to fuck. Her touch was strong and confident, her body on fire and inviting. Gio surrendered himself to the sensations, the thrill of the forbidden mixing with their undeniable attraction.

As the night wore on, they found themselves wrapped in sheets, their bodies entwined, the city silent outside. Gio struggled to remember the last time he was this excited, immersed in a moment. Valentina rested beside him, her head on his chest, their breaths slowly becoming evener.

"Thank you for tonight," she murmured, her fingers gently drawing shapes on his skin. "I needed this."

Gio smiled, his hand moving through her hair. "I needed it, too."

The connection they shared was brief, yet genuine. Rome had gifted them this night, a short escape from the demands and expectations of their everyday lives. As they fell asleep, Gio realized this was a night he would cherish forever.

Morning came sooner than expected, ushering in the reality of the Ryder Cup and their shared world. As they parted ways, Valentina gave Gio a lingering kiss and a promise to reunite.

Once again, Rome had worked its magic. It had taken Gio on a journey through its streets, tales, and people, leaving him with enduring memories. As he returned to the course, prepared for the final day of matches, Gio's step was lighter and more connected to the city that had given him so much.

Chapter 21

Crossroads

The singles match played out just as expected, and when the clinching putt fell, the crowd burst into a wave of excitement that echoed across the course.

The European team achieved the win. They had secured the Ryder Cup.

Flags waved, chants filled the atmosphere, and the players hugged each other, their faces showing a blend of relief and joy. It was a historic victory, and Franco was right in the middle.

Gio stood on the sidelines with a rush of pride and admiration. Franco was nothing short of astounding; his performance was as sharp as the cheers that erupted after each of his shots. The Italian had taken the team lead, his calmness under pressure and relentless determination made him the day's standout.

The already devoted crowd started chanting his name with a passion usually reserved for soccer legends. "Fra-an-co! Fra-an-co!" they shouted, their voices blending into a mighty chorus of praise.

Gio was swept up in the moment's emotion as the celebrations kicked into high gear. He had covered countless events and witnessed unforgettable victories, but this was different. Perhaps it was the setting—Rome, a city that seemed to pulse with passion—or maybe it was the people, from the players to the fans, who had infused this Ryder Cup with a spirit that few others could match.

Gio turned and watched Franco being lifted onto his teammates' shoulders, a broad smile illuminating his face. He had become a national hero overnight, and the pride in his eyes was unmistakable. Gio felt a pang of something—indeed, admiration and a hint of envy. Franco had accomplished something monumental, something that would be remembered for years to come.

As the evening wore on, the celebrations overflowed from the course into the streets of Rome. The city had taken the victory to heart, with impromptu parties springing up in Campo de Fiori, Trastevere, and the grand Piazza Navona, wine flowing, and strangers bonding in the collective happiness of the occasion.

When the initial thrill of victory faded into a more contemplative atmosphere, Gio found himself at a pivotal moment. The Ryder Cup had concluded, and his travel assignment was completed. The pressing question now was: What would he do next?

Gio strolled through the winding streets, the sounds of celebration still resonating in the background, his mind drifting back to La Terre Felice and Gabby. The Tuscan estate had served as his refuge for many months, a haven where he could escape the world's chaos, write in tranquility, and savor the simple joys of life with the woman he cherished. It was his place of renewal, where he discovered clarity and inspiration. The thought of returning was reassuring, like slipping into a favorite old coat.

Yet, Rome had ignited something within him: a restlessness and a desire to explore. The city had rekindled the excitement of wandering and embracing the unknown, and he was unwilling to let that go.

Europe was expansive, filled with countless places he had yet to explore and so many stories waiting to be uncovered. The prospect of continuing his journey, of allowing the road to guide him, was enticing.

He stood on a bridge overlooking the Tiber, the river shimmering with the city lights. The decision lay before him: Return to the comfort of La Terre Felice or venture once more into the unknown and see where his travels might take him.

Gio leaned against the railing, the fantastic night breeze brushing against his face as he contemplated his choices. La Terre Felice represented safety, a grounding place, but staying there would mean leaving behind the thrill and spontaneity he had experienced in recent days.

Continuing to roam through Europe meant embracing uncertainty and opening the door to new adventures, fresh experiences, and more connections. But he would abandon his dream of a future with Gabby.

Franco's triumph served as a reminder of what could be accomplished when one pursued one's passion; perhaps that was the lesson Gio needed to carry forward. Whether he chose to return to La Terre Felice or continue his wanderings, the important thing was to remain true to himself and follow the path that called to him most.

As Gio stood there, the distant sound of a cathedral chiming, he realized he didn't have to decide immediately. Life flowed on its journey, and he learned to trust the current long ago. He could now enjoy the moment, savor the European team's victory, and let the night guide him.

Gio turned away from the river, smiling, and started walking, lighter on his feet than in years. For the first time in a long while, he felt at ease. The world was vast, and he was ready to welcome whatever he stumbled upon.

As the night sky unfolded above Gio, he understood one thing for sure: His story was about to take a turn as he saw a figure approaching.

Chapter 22

A Twist of Fate

It was Valentina. She had searched for him all evening, radiating her fiery aura from every pore.

"It was a glorious day, Gio," she said. "I have only one thing on my mind right now. Let's go to my place."

Gio was ready, too, and quick to oblige. Valentina's suite was nestled within one of Rome's most exclusive hotels and positioned for discreet meetings and covert activities.

The hotel was a masterpiece of luxury, with its grand facade and prime location offering views of historic landmarks. Valentina's suite sat high above the bustling streets, providing a private sanctuary away from prying eyes while still at the center of Rome's vibrant energy.

Upon returning, they ordered a bottle of Nero D'avola Sicilian red. Valentina poured, and Gio sipped while watching her undress. She was a sight to behold—hot. Before he could indulge fully, a strange lightheadedness overtook him, like blood rushing out of his body. His mind raced, and he concluded that Valentina had slipped something into his glass of wine ...

Chapter 23

Bad Bogey Discretion

A loud bang on the door awakened Gio. It was morning, and he had no memory after that first sip of wine until the morning light. Valentina was nowhere to be found.

Two burly goons were waiting to slap duct tape across Gio's mouth and zip-tie his hands together.

"Giulio Mazocca wants to see you," said the larger of the two men, whose barrel chest almost knocked Gio to the ground. 'We're taking you to him."

Gio was familiar with the Mazocca name, having written articles about the land baron and investigating his shady dealings in grabbing property from working-class families across Sicily and mainland Italy, among other illegal and unethical behavior. Connected to a long line of influential land barons in Sicily, Giulio inherited confiscated land and was part of a complex web of alliances and rivalries that came with property.

His family's suspected ties to organized crime were an open secret, giving him leverage and enemies. Giulio's upbringing was steeped in underworld power struggles, shaping him into a ruthless leader who stopped at nothing to protect his interests.

The entourage transported Gio by helicopter and high-speed boat to Mazocca's luxurious but isolated island off the coast of Malta. The island was a symphony of nature, accessible only by private transportation. It rose dramatically from crystal-clear waters, its highest point crowned by a lavish and secure compound that offered sweeping views of the Mediterranean Sea. Hidden coves and dense groves provided natural barriers, ensuring privacy and seclusion for Mazocca and his empire.

The burly men pushed Gio into a large room, where Mazocca was waiting.

"I've been watching your travel escapades and reading you for a long time," Mazocca snarled. "Your writing sucks. The stakes have been raised for you now, and the tables have turned, writer boy. I'm prepared to expose many things I know you don't want known. I've got some dark secrets about La Terre Felice, too. You wouldn't want to see your girlfriend's property ownership invalidated, would you?"

"You're a monster, you son of a bitch," Gio raged.

"That I am, my friend. That I am."

Mazocca presented an old document proving that La Terre Felice belonged to his ancestors, the Sicilian nobility, who were forced out under suspicious circumstances centuries ago. His speech was commanding and cutting, marked by a strong Sicilian dialect. He spoke without embellishment, getting straight to the point. "If this information was brought to the Italian courts, the property would be returned to my family, and I would own La Terre Felice," Mazocca said. "I know you don't want me to do that—though I hear your girlfriend isn't too happy with you right now. I need to know what dirt you've got on me in those spiral notebooks you writers all seem to use."

"That will never happen," Gio replied hastily.

Just then, Valentina entered the room. Gio's heart sank as realization dawned.

Chapter 24

Ties to Corruption

Giulio Mazocca was powerful and influential. His sharp features and brusque, direct demeanor intimidated and instilled fear in anyone who crossed his path. His air of authority was difficult to ignore.

Mazocca controlled influential figures in local government and organized crime. His empire stretched across various sectors, and his far-reaching influence garnered him both fear and respect.

"I have deep connections with the Ryder Cup community," Mazocca said, his anger intensifying his Sicilian accent. "I control the media and can manipulate coverage to damage your reputation, leaving you persona non grata in golf and travel writing forever. If you don't cooperate, I'll ruin your life *and* your buddy Franco's life, making you both disappear."

"My mistake," Gio said. "This was a setup, and I'm a moron for not seeing it." He turned his attention to Valentina and said, "I should've known. You were too hot and easy."

Valentina strode toward Gio and slapped him across the face. "I am my father's daughter," she said. "You mess with me; you mess with him."

Of course. A seducer and a spy. She sure didn't get her looks and charm from her father the thug though, Gio thought.

Despite being in a dangerous, hopeless situation, Gio held one card that Mazocca didn't know about: a cache of documents from his investigative work safely hidden in the digital cloud that exposed Mazocca's corrupt activities as a land baron and linked him to several high-profile unsolved murders in Sicily. The deaths had been labeled as accidents or disappearances, but Gio's investigations connected them directly to Mazocca's empire. If this information were made public, Mazocca would lose his power and face a lifetime in prison.

As Gio pondered the shitstorm he had created thanks to his lack of discretion, he couldn't help but want to be back at La Terre Felice with Gabby, a place of safety and peacefulness. Then his thoughts shifted to Franco, who clearly was also in danger.

As if Mazocca read Gio's mind, he roared, "Your pal Franco is on his way. I know you better than you know yourself."

Chapter 25

The Deal

The following day, Gio was under careful watch by Mazocca's bodyguards, Eastern Europeans with menacing looks. Hearing footsteps outside the door, Gio looked up to see Franco being led in by one of Mazocca's goons. Franco's stern, perplexed gaze burned a hole through Gio as he arrived.

Mazocca, certainly a man of questionable morals, presented Gio with a final test, "Face off against my hand-picked golfing prodigy, Alessandro, whose talent rivals that of the world's best young pro golfers. If you lose, you must immediately have Gabriella Rosetti sign over ownership of La Terre Felice and never expose my secrets. If you win, I'll destroy the ancient land deeds and leave La Terre Felice untouched."

"However, there is a catch," noted Giulio. "If you use any information uncovered during your investigation against me, I'll have you killed."

"Oh yes, we know about that," Valentina added. "Don't look so surprised, you idiot."

"In return, I will donate five million euro to a Tuscany preservation fund, provided the land surrounding La Terre Felice remains safe from future development or seizure."

Well, sure that benefits your family, too, Gio thought wryly.

Once Mazocca and the guards left the room, Franco recognized that Gio had gotten himself in too deep and that once again, he must take care of business.

"What about this, Gio," Franco said. "We can use my knowledge of Mazocca's connections to organized crime and the confiscation of land owned by my parents in Viterbo."

Franco proposed a side bet. "If you win, Gio, with me on the bag, we reclaim ownership of La Terre Felice and force Mazocca to cut ties with all the land he confiscated."

Even if Giulio disagrees, we have him, Franco noted, having gathered evidence of Mazocca's criminal activities against his family years ago.

Franco then shared with Gio valuable insights into a young player's weaknesses on the course. Together, they devised a risky plan to outsmart Alessandro in a high-stakes game that would take place the next day on the island.

Chapter 26

The Golf Hustle

Despite Valentina's short time with Gio, she had developed feelings for him and did not want to see him destroyed. Her father's pressure to continue the family corruption and violence had taken a toll on her. She was weary of seducing men for her father and tired of the lifestyle.

Without her father's knowledge, she contacted Gio the night before the big match, offering to help sabotage her father's plans by preparing a special energy cocktail for Alessandro and providing inside information on her father's strategies and vulnerabilities.

"Why should I trust you now?" Gio exclaimed.

"You don't have much choice, do you, Gio?"

The golf match occurred on the island in a breathtaking yet precarious setting. The meticulously maintained course stretched along rolling hills and plush fairways, punctuated by strategically placed bunkers and water hazards that reflected the azure sky and competed with the blue waters surrounding the island.

At the start, the air was crisp and clean, carrying Mediterranean breezes that cooled the skin under the hot sun. Tensions ran high as Mazocca's goons watched from the sidelines. Gio and Franco employed their calculated strategies, but Alessandro was an almost unbeatable opponent on his home course. Going into the eighteenth hole, the match was all square.

When all seemed lost, a storm brewed. The weather became symbolic of the turmoil surrounding Gio and Mazocca. The last hole played through heavy rain was more of a psychological battleground than a physical one. With Franco's timely advice and a crucial pulled drive slip-up from Alessandro—possibly aided by Valentina's undercover intervention—Gio sank the winning putt to win the match.

With the game over, Gio learned that Alessandro, the golf prodigy, was Giulio's son and Valentina's younger brother.

"I knew who Alessandro was," Franco admitted after the match. "He received a few exemptions to play in tournament events last year. He will be a great pro one day, but Gio, you know this game is won or lost between the ears. It's all about mental toughness."

"And Valentina went against her blood," Gio responded. "That's a cardinal sin in any organized crime family. I'll deal with you later, *paisan,* for keeping that knowledge from me."

She is part of this mess now, Gio thought.

Before Gio could leave the course, Mazocca came striding up toward him. Distraught that this hustler, Gio, defeated his rising prodigy, he yelled, "*Buttana di to mà!* I'm bound to uphold my end of the deal—if you're lucky that is."

"Ha! You don't even know the half of it," Gio said. "With a computer inside your compound in an unlocked hallway, I accessed incriminating documents and sent them to national media, Interpol, and international organized crime law enforcement. They'll be on to you very soon," Gio said smugly.

"*Bastardu!*" screamed the Sicilian. "I should feed you both to the sharks." Mazocca was backed into a corner. His empire would be destroyed if Gio and Franco suffered retaliation. Public and government scrutiny would be severe. Valentina, complicit yet sympathetic toward Gio, needed to side with her father.

Defeated and humiliated, Mazocca retreated. In the coming weeks, his whole operation was exposed, and he was indicted for lifelong crimes. La Terre Felice was saved. Although Gio emerged victorious and with his integrity intact, the experience and Valentina's betrayal left lasting scars.

As Gio and Franco departed the compound and helped themselves to the high-speed boat,

Gio's irreverence was more for Valentina. "You think Sicilians are so tough, so smart," he said to her. "Remember, don't ever fuck with a *Napulitan!*"

Chapter 27

An Unsung Hero

On returning to La Terre Felice following their recent escapade to Mazocca's island, Gio made a pact with Franco, "We can't divulge anything to Gabby," Gio said with his heart in his throat. "It would be too tragic to tell her how close she came to losing La Terre Felice. I am such an idiot, a fool. I could have lost everything for her."

"Sono d'accordo," Franco added.

In the aftermath of the experience, Gio collaborated with his contacts to ensure the property in Tuscany was entirely under the Rosetti family's ownership, and he still was able to secure that large donation for the Tuscany Preservation Fund. Franco's family received their land deeded back to them, and any remaining land ownership gaps were eliminated forever.

While Gio drove back to La Terre Felice from Rome, he received a call from Gabby, who has not been feeling well.

"Gabby, you sound tired," Gio said. "You're working yourself too hard. I know the estate is a lot of responsibility."

"The fatigue and physical weakness come and go. They especially rear up when I'm stressed," Gabby said.

"How long has this been happening?" Gio asked. "Why didn't you tell me before?"

"It's a bit chronic, and I generally get over the problem quickly."

"Have you seen any doctors about it? We should address this further," Gio said, still mostly unaware that Gabby was already under doctors' care. "Franco and I are on the drive back. We'll see you later this evening, okay? *Ciao, bella.*"

In the passenger's seat, Franco mulled over Gio's side of the conversation. He had kept his word to Gabby, never telling Gio about her worsening condition. Franco met Gabby soon after she first met Gio, and he had witnessed difficulties in their relationship. He had always admired Gio's passion for his work, but he recognized its strain on the relationship with Gabby.

"Gio, we share unique challenges in our lives," Franco said to his friend. "You as a journalist and me as an athlete."

Gio nodded in agreement.

"Both of our careers demand total commitment," Franco added. "Often at the expense of relationships."

Franco and Gio shared a peaceful drive-time chat. Franco began talking about the difficulty he's had in managing his personal life and career. "This life is a sacrifice," he said. "My relationships have suffered from my commitment to golf. I admit: I have regrets. Sometimes I wish I had put the people who mattered most first."

Franco turned to Gio and asked, "How about you? Your relationship with Gabby seems precarious at best. If you don't make a change, put her first, you might lose her. Success and adventure are essential, but they are empty without someone to share them with."

Franco knew how much Gabby meant to Gio. He encouraged Gio to be there for her. "Maybe it's time to find a new way of living. How can you pursue your passions but not at the cost of the woman you love."

Gio felt a shift deep within himself. "Maybe you're right," he said. "Maybe my life doesn't have to be an all-or-nothing decision. Perhaps there's a way for my love for Gabby and my passion for work to thrive together."

Chapter 28

Mother and Daughter

That afternoon, Gabby and Antoinette relaxed on the farmhouse porch, gazing out at the vineyard. They were grateful for some peace and quiet, having just wrapped up a hectic day of greeting and tending to guests and preparing and serving dinner.

The atmosphere was peaceful, yet tense because both women were aware of Gabby's worsening health issues, even though they rarely talked about them. A beautiful, vibrant woman was suffering, her body under attack from the inside.

Gabby remained determined to fulfill her work commitments despite her health, not wanting to burden Antoinette or jeopardize the success of La Terre Felice. As the disease progressed, it began to take a significant toll on her body. Instead of providing protection, her immune system started attacking her internal organs.

She sought the necessary medical help, but the autoimmune disease was relentless. Although new treatments offered some relief, there was no cure, and the disease continued to advance. At times, Gabby experienced phases of remission, during which her body behaved normally, only for the disease to flare up again, each time more intense.

By Gabby's mid-thirties, the disease began to compromise her ability to fight off infections, leading to more frequent illnesses. Even a simple cold could escalate into something much more severe. Gabby tried to stay involved at La Terre Felice, but there were moments when she had to step back, leaving Antoinette and the staff to take on more responsibilities.

"The guests seemed especially happy today," Antoinette said sipping her *caffe*. "I saw them taking pictures by the old olive tree. That couple from Milan couldn't stop talking about your tour this morning."

"It's nice to see people enjoying the place," Gabby responded with tired eyes. "Seeing their faces light up when they savor the wine or the view from the top of the hill makes all of the hard work worth it."

Antoinette nodded. "You're doing a beautiful job with them, Gabby. La Terre Felice epitomizes you. But please know that you don't have to do everything. We can hire more help if you need it."

"No. I want to do this. It keeps me going. Seeing the guests happy … it helps. And besides, no one can bring out the welcome mat like we do. This place is our heart, Mamma. It's personal."

"I get it, but I'm anxious about you. You've been working too hard. I can see it, Gabby. I know you're not feeling well."

"I am fine. This place … it's what I have now. It keeps me connected to Gio, even if he's not here. And I can't let it fall apart just because I'm a little tired," Gabby said, tears welling up. "I need to make sure this place is perfect, for the guests and for us. And maybe, just maybe, one day, if Gio wants to stay forever, he'll see what we've built here—what I've built for us."

Gabby gazed out into the distance before she continued, "It's hard though. I miss him every day he's away. And I'm scared that if I stop, let go even a little bit … it will fall apart. That I'll fall apart."

"Gabby, I'm here, and so is everyone else who loves you. We'll keep La Terre Felice thriving together. But we need you to be okay, too. That's what matters most," Antoinette said.

"I just want him to come home for good. But I know he won't, not yet. So I must ensure this place is all we dreamed it could be."

"We'll make it everything and more, Gabby. But promise me you'll take care of yourself. We're in this together, okay?"

"Okay. I promise. But please know I'm so grateful for all of your hard work, too. The guests can't stop raving about your food. They claim it's the best they've ever had."

Then mother and daughter drifted off to their own private, peaceful thoughts, knowing that no matter what challenges arose, La Terre Felice would symbolize their resilience, love, and the life they've created together—even amidst heartache and uncertainty.

Chapter 29

The Return

Gio and Franco's arrival back at La Terre Felice infused Gabby with a surge of energy. She greeted the pair with the typical Italian woman warmth—open arms, hugs, kisses, and some vino. The three sat together on an outside terrace, all with much on their minds.

"*Grandi congratulazioni*, Franco. You are the new Italian celebrity," Gabby toasted.

"*Tante grazie*," said the new Italian star, as they all raised glasses of the finest bottle of Felice wine.

"So special, so peaceful," Gio said.

After the last drop of wine was savored, Franco, sensing Gabby and Gio needed some time to reconnect, retired to a cottage, where he planned to stay for the night.

Gio and Gabby sat for a few moments in silence.

Gio broke the spell, "Gabby, I've been doing a lot of thinking, searching for the right answers for us," he said.

"Gio, I care so much for you, and I want us to be happy together," Gabby replied, clearly upset and tearing up.

"I promise, Gabby. I've had a change of heart. I'm going to break from my nomadic life. I want to help you and your mamma with La Terre Felice," Gio said.

As if Gio was looking at La Terre Felice with fresh eyes, he saw it transform from a chained burden into a refuge, where he found healing and reflection, both much needed after his brush with death with Mazocca. As Gio immersed himself in working the vineyard—tending to the grapes, overseeing the harvest, and assisting with wine production—he discovered a new sense of fulfillment. The peaceful routine of working alongside Gabby, Antoinette, and the staff offered him a fresh perspective on life.

"I want to learn how to identify the best grapes for harvesting and understand how these fruits and vegetables flourish to their peak ripeness," Gio told Luca. "Antoinette expects the best for her cooking. I don't want to disappoint her."

"You better get it right, Giovanni," Luca scolded. "Otherwise she might look for that rolling pin again." The two men roared with laughter at that visual.

Throughout the next few months, as Gabby and Gio shared the tranquil moments of vineyard life, they grew closer and more connected. Gio enjoyed the stability of living far from the chaos of his usual travels. Feeling more at peace and stable with Gio back home, Gabby's health stabilized, and their time together allowed them to reconnect deeper. Antoinette also valued Gio's presence because he brought renewed energy to the estate and helped lighten her load.

However, as time passed, the addiction to the open road and world beyond La Terre Felice began to stir again within Gio. Despite the peace he had found and his deep love for Gabby, restlessness started once more. The familiar urge to explore, chase stories, and experience life in all its forms grew stronger each day.

One evening, as the sun dipped below the vineyard's rolling hills, Gio sat down with Gabby for a heartfelt conversation. He expressed the significance of the past months for both, highlighting how being there for her and working at La Terre Felice has given him a new outlook on life.

But the outside world still called to him, and he desired to respond to that pull. He had been offered the opportunity of a lifetime to cover the Italian national team at the upcoming Summer Olympics in Paris.

Deciding to leave La Terre Felice was difficult, and when Gio revealed his plans to Gabby, it triggered an intense argument for the first time in their relationship.

Gio gathered his courage to bring up the topic. They sat on the farmhouse porch, the tranquil beauty of the day's twilight sharply contrasting with the brewing storm between them. Gabby sensed his unease, but the conversation still caught her off guard.

"I've been thinking—" Gio began, his voice shaky, "I think it's time for me to leave again. This opportunity is historical and offers so many stories to tell."

Gabby turned to him, her expression hardening in anticipation of what she had been dreading. "You want to leave? Again? After everything we've been through? After everything I've endured?"

Gio shifted in his seat, searching for the right words. "It's not about leaving you, Gabby. You know how much you mean to me, how much this place means to me. But I can't do it here—staying in one place—not yet. There's a part of me that still needs to explore, to discover—"

Gabby interrupted, her voice rising in anger. "What am I supposed to do? Just wait for you to get tired of wandering? What about everything we've built together? Doesn't that matter to you?"

"It means everything," Gio insisted, growing exasperated that she couldn't see his perspective. "But this is who I am. I could stay and settle down, but I'm not ready. It's suffocating me, Gabby."

"Suffocating you?" Gabby repeated, incredulous. "Is that how you see this? As a prison? After all my sacrifices and the time we've spent trying to make this work, you tell me you feel trapped?"

Gio's frustration reached a boiling point. "You don't understand, Gabby! It's not about you or this place. It's what I need to feel alive. I can't just turn that off because you want me to. You knew who I was when we met. You accepted this was part of me."

Gabby stood and paced the porch, her emotions a whirlwind of anger, hurt, and disappointment. "I knew who you were, but I thought you would want more—want us. But it's always been about what you need. What about what I need, Gio? I need you here with me. I need someone willing to stay."

The words lingered in the air, and for a moment, all was quiet. Then Gio stood, his anger fading as he acknowledged the pain in Gabby's eyes.

"I love you, Gabby," he said softly. "But I can't be someone I'm not. If I stay, I'll only resent this situation. And I don't want that. I don't want us to end up hating each other."

Gabby's eyes filled with tears. She blinked back at them, refusing to cry. "And what if you leave and never come back? What then, Gio? What if I'm just not enough to make you stay?"

Gio stepped closer, reaching out as Gabby pulled away. "You are enough," he said with sincerity. "But this isn't just about that. It's about discovering who I am and what I'm meant to do. I promise I'll return, but I must do this."

Gabby shook her head, her voice quivering under the weight of her feelings. "Maybe one day you'll see that what you're searching for has been here all along. But I can't keep waiting, Gio. I can't keep pausing my life for someone who can't decide what he wants."

A long silence stretched between them, both sensing that this conversation has again altered something essential in their relationship. Gabby turned away, with her arms wrapped around herself as if trying to hold everything together.

Gio looked at her, his heart heavy with regret and love, before he turned and walked away, knowing that this might be the hardest goodbye he's ever had to face.

As Gio left the porch and headed back inside, Gabby remained behind, tears flowing. She was losing Gio all over again. And this time, she's uncertain if he'll ever return.

Chapter 30

The Relapse

After Gio left La Terre Felice for Paris, the emotional toll of their argument and his departure weighed heavily on Gabby. The stress and heartbreak triggered a relapse of her illness in the days that followed, something she had hoped to avoid.

As Gabby's health deteriorated, she became determined once again not to burden Gio with the news, knowing how much it would hurt him and fearing that he might force himself to return out of guilt rather than love.

Despite the pleas of Antoinette and the close-knit community at the vineyard, she remained adamant that Gio must not be informed. She wanted him to continue his journey without the weight of her illness pulling him back. Gabby believed that if Gio returned because of her condition, it would only reinforce the idea that he was sacrificing his happiness for her, which she didn't want.

"Gabby, it's time for you to inform Gio of the seriousness of your illness," Antoinette insisted.

"He needs to understand that his actions are impacting your health, whether you believe that or not. Every time he leaves, your body triggers a relapse. This is not good, *cara*."

"Mamma, I cannot force Gio to give up his passion in life," Gabby responded. "Only he can resolve what's most important. I know my strong feelings for him to be here brings on more stress and would force him to sacrifice his happiness."

"But what about your happiness, Gabby? You deserve it more than anyone."

Even Franco, Gio's best friend and confidant, who was on the road traveling and playing in tour events since his visit to La Terre Felice after the Ryder Cup, stayed updated on Gabby's latest relapse.

Despite Franco's deep concern for Gabby, he continued to honor her wishes, though it pained him to stay silent. He was torn between his loyalty to Gabby and his friendship with Gio, knowing how devastated Gio would be if he found out. Franco, who had seen the impact of their relationship on both, struggled with his promise to Gabby.

Chapter 31

The Clueless Wanderlust

Over the next few weeks, Gabby's illness continued to progress. She leaned more and more on her mother and their staff. Franco, back in the area for a much needed rest, provided a calm, reassuring sounding board, but Gabby steadfastly refused to bring Gio back into her circle of trust.

After leaving La Terre Felice, Gio flew to Paris to cover the Olympics. He stayed near the Champs Élysées and enjoyed a carefree single trip in the City of Lights, including the experience of the opening ceremony that showcased the athletes' parade of nations on the Seine River along with the wonder of the Eiffel Tower illuminated at night.

The participating Italian national team was formidable, and while they were winning medals, Gio didn't miss an opportunity to savor the French wine and delicacies that Paris is known to offer any discerning traveler.

After the closing Olympics ceremony, Gio experienced the highs and lows of his wanderlust life. He had moments of immense satisfaction, like when he published a well-received article or discovered a hidden vacation paradise. But there were also moments of loneliness and restlessness when the excitement of travel and women was not enough to fill the void left by his absence from home.

When Gio returned to La Terre Felice in between his travels with a verbal commitment to permanently stay with Gabby, the call for more adventure counter-punched him like an addictive endorphin drug feeding a restless desire for more exploration and experiences in life.

During these visits, Gio spent time working with and supporting the staff, almost like a psychological cleansing, while reconnecting with Gabby and Antoinette. But those times were brief, usually a few weeks or months, and he never lingered long enough to see the impact that Gabby's illness was having on her. Always the optimist, Gabby would wear a brave face, minimizing her symptoms and concentrating on making the most of their moments together.

Chapter 32

Rallying Around the Beautiful Soul

Gabby's latest relapse made her even more aware of the time she wished to spend with Gio, not just in fleeting moments between his travels. Her need for him to be by her side became a matter of love and necessity. She longed to have someone to lean on, share her burden, and support her through the challenges ahead.

Antoinette and their staff all understood the unspoken truth—that Gio, the person she loves most, had no idea what was happening. The vineyard continued to function, but there was an underlying sadness as they watched Gabby's strength wane without the support of the one person she wanted by her side. Even Gabby's doctors urged her to find a steady, long-term presence, a partner who would always be there.

As Gabby's illness progressed, the workers at La Terre Felice stepped up in countless ways. Luca, Maria, Paolo, Sofia, and Giuseppe all took on additional duties without complaint, often working late into the night to ensure everything was in order. They also provided emotional support to Gabby and Antoinette, understanding the weight of the situation and doing their best to lighten the load.

Maria stepped up to help Sofia with guest relations and to schedule visitors for their day-trip exploration and tours of various historical churches and towns. Luca and Paolo mixed their teams to accommodate the demands of the farm and cultivating the vineyards, while Pino took over for Gabby in harvesting and cleaning the best vegetables from the garden for Antoinette's meal preparation.

Their loyalty and dedication were instrumental in keeping La Terre Felice thriving during such a difficult period. They worked as a team, each contributing their unique skills and strengths to ensure that the *agriturismo* remained a place of warmth, comfort, and hospitality for every guest.

Chapter 33

A Broken Promise

After holding back for what felt like forever, Franco decided to inform Gio about Gabby's declining health. Franco had been holding onto Gabby's secret for too long, witnessing her gradual decline while Gio remained in the dark about how serious her illness was. Franco found the weight of that secret unbearable. He had to tell Gio the truth, even if it meant risking Gabby's trust.

I know Gabby will understand, but Gio will not like this at all," Franco thought on the way to meet his friend. *Gabby needs Gio more than ever. He owes her his undivided attention, love, and support, and I owe her my loyalty to help. Telling Gio shows my respect for both of them.*

The fateful conversation happened in Rome, where Franco attended a charity golf event. The two met for what Gio assumed would be a casual catch-up over drinks. But Franco was tense, and his usual lighthearted demeanor was replaced by a somber seriousness that Gio couldn't ignore.

After a few minutes of light banter, Franco couldn't keep it in any longer. He looked Gio in the eye and said, "Gio, there's something you need to know about Gabby."

Gio's heart dropped. The way Franco spoke and the pause before his words made it clear that what was coming wouldn't be good news. "What's up?" he asked, dreading Franco's reply.

"Gabby's autoimmune disease had progressed," Franco began. "She's been battling it by herself. She had asked me not to tell you because she didn't want to interfere with your life."

At first, Gio was in disbelief, struggling to process the information. But as Franco kept talking, his shock turned into anger. "I can't believe you, of all people, kept this from me," Gio fumed. His anger escalated into an intense argument, emotions spilling over in a way neither had expected. "How could you not tell me, Franco? She's my family, too! I had a right to know!" Gio shouted, his voice trembling with a mix of rage and guilt.

Franco, upset, shot back, "Do you think I wanted to keep this from you? Gabby made me promise! She didn't want to trap you, Gio. She didn't want you to drop everything and return."

"*She* didn't want that? Or *you* didn't want that?" Gio retorted, his mind racing with accusations and regret. "You should have told me, Franco. I could have been there for her.

Instead, I've been out running all about, wasting time while she suffers!"

Franco's frustration boiled over. "You think you could have been there? Gio, you've explored so many places, chasing your dreams! She didn't want to stand in your way; maybe she was right. But don't pin everything on me. You know she's always put others before herself!"

The argument continued with both men saying things they might not have under different circumstances. Franco kept his helplessness and guilt in check for a while, then unleashed his anger. Reeling from the revelation and guilt, Gio responded with an emotional outburst.

The argument broke, and both men realized they were hurting each other more than helping Gabby by fighting. The room fell silent, and the weight of the situation settled like a heavy weight between them.

Franco, his voice hoarse from shouting, spoke softly. "Gio, I'm sorry. I know I should have told you sooner. But we both know Gabby. She wanted you to live your life, not to be tied down by her illness. But it isn't good now, Gio. You need to go back home to her."

Gio, still reeling from the confrontation, nodded slowly. The anger was still there, but it was now blended with urgency and guilt. He recognized that Franco was right. He had to see Gabby—before it was too late.

Without another word, Gio got up and left, his mind racing with thoughts of Gabby and the time he had lost. Franco watched him go, regretful but relieved to know the truth had finally been revealed.

Chapter 34

The Awakening

After arguing with Franco, Gio wasted no time returning to La Terre Felice. The shock and guilt fueled his determination to be there for Gabby and make up for lost time.

Gio called and texted Gabby on the drive from Rome. The call immediately went to voicemail and his texts were unanswered. His concern and worry intensified.

Over the past few weeks, Gabby's disease had progressed. Most days, she confined herself in bed with her favorite quilt pulled up to her chin for warmth—and comfort. She had lost quite a bit of weight, and her once radiant beauty suffered. Most days she didn't even have the energy to eat. Antoinette worked her best culinary magic to try to tempt her, but to no avail.

When Gio arrived, the sight of Gabby's failing figure, weakened by the disease, filled him with an overwhelming mix of emotions—relief that he was there, sorrow for what she had endured due to his stubborn Italian ways, and a fierce resolve to do whatever it took to help her.

The Gabby Gio now saw was a slighter, paler version of the beauty he had met just a few years prior. Gabby's skin was pale, her piercing blue eyes sunken. It pained Gio's heart to see her look this way, only imagining how she must feel. For Gio, this turned into a moment of profound introspection. He loved Gabby, and the thought of her suffering was unbearable.

Gabby's health crisis forced Gio to confront the realities that life is short and unpredictable and the future he's always chased might not be worth as much without the person who's been waiting for him to come home. The situation pushed Gio to reconsider his priorities as he grappled with the possibility of losing Gabby.

To everyone's surprise and relief, shortly after Gio returned, Gabby went into remission again. The timing seemed miraculous, as if her body responded to his presence, giving them one last chance to make things right.

Gabby's skin color and appetite returned—much to the delight of Antoinette. She regained some of her strength and once again tended to the needs of the *agriturismo*. It was as if the cloud of illness had lifted for a time. Together with Antoinette and the loyal workers of La Terre Felice, Gabby experienced a period of renewed hope.

"Gabby, as God is my witness and in front of the Madonna Mary, I will not leave you or La

Terre Felice again," Gio vowed. "I am committed forever!"

Gabby was mesmerized. While her blue eyes intensified and pointed like lasers ready to fire, she asked herself, *Can I finally believe this nomad? He swore an oath to God. Now I'm gonna have a front-row seat every day."*

With Gabby better, Gio threw himself into enhancing La Terre Felice. He understood this was where he belonged—not just for Gabby, but for himself. The nomadic lifestyle that once seemed so enticing now turned empty compared to the fulfillment he discovered in his efforts to improve and preserve the place that held such significance for him and her family.

Just as Gio made peace with his decision, he received an inquiry from the British Broadcasting Company (BBC) in America. The media giant wanted his unbiased coverage of the upcoming national election in the United States. America would elect its next President in November, and this type of reporting and traveling across the US would catapult Gio into the stratosphere internationally.

Gio's mind raced on the conversation with himself.

I know Gabby would believe this is a phenomenal opportunity, and in better times, she might tell me to go. But I also know she needs me here now, and she is watching to see if I will break my promise to her. Franco always said it's not just about the next win, but more importantly, it's about the relationships that are lasting. I know what I'm going to do.

After a few sleepless nights, Gio summoned the courage to talk to Gabby after lunch.

"Bella, I want to be completely honest with you to prove I'm worthy of your trust and loyalty," Gio started. "I was offered to go to America to cover the presidential election for the BBC. I turned it down."

Gabby was stunned into silence.

"Say something, anything," Gio said.

"Wow, Gio! That's *incredible!*" Gabby gushed. "You must be over the moon with the offer. It would also allow you to reconnect with your mamma, Isabella. That would be important for you, Gio."

"Yes, Bella. Important work and reconnection for sure," Gio said. "But right here and now, my place is with you. All that matters is for us to be together."

Gabby was speechless as she left to walk in the vineyards.

With his decision final, Gio began to infuse La Terre Felice with a fresh perspective, blending the traditional charm that had always defined it with innovative ideas to attract a wider audience.

Growing up in America, Gio knew the romantic draw that Italy had on people. For those who have traveled to and experienced the charm of the Italian countryside and its hilltop villages, the tales of exquisite food, local wine, and storied history were abundant.

For those who have yet to experience Italy, it becomes a personal bucket list item. Gio knew that and enlisted Sofia's expertise in using data analytics to better target prospective business for La Terre Felice.

"We have to keep the pipeline filled, Sofia," Gio said. "That's a captive audience to nurture and convert to experience our lifestyle. They will come back again and again."

Drawing from his global travels, Gio initiated new elements that distinguished the *agriturismo* as the premier pure Tuscan destination.

Gio offered a variety of activities for guests, including guided tours to nearby hilltop villages, local vineyards, horseback riding through the countryside, and hot-air balloon rides over the picturesque hills and valleys of Tuscany. For more adventurous guests, Gio organized excursions to Sicily's hot spots like Cefalu, a northern coastal town on the island; Palermo, where rich traditions exude from every dusty corner, including theatrical events at the Palermo Opera House made famous in Godfather III; and Taormina, a posh resort town on the east coast nestled at the foot of Mount Etna. Each activity was crafted to highlight Sicily's spectacular beauty and diverse culture.

Gio also collaborated closely with Luca to enhance the vineyards and olive groves, implementing sustainable methods to increase their output, by furthering Luca's expertise in soil management, irrigation, pruning techniques, and organic pest control. They started producing more high-quality wines and olive oils—thanks to Gio's culinary connections throughout Europe, which earned acclaim among connoisseurs and were sold at La Terre Felice's lobby *enoteca*.

With Antoinette and Pino leading the way in the kitchen, Gio expanded the culinary offerings at La Terre Felice—drawing from his vast experience wining and dining on his travels. They introduced seasonal tasting menus and specialty cooking classes that attracted food lovers and chefs from all over.

Gio collaborated with Sofia and Maria, too, to enhance the guest accommodations, merging rustic Tuscan features with contemporary comforts. They redesigned private villas, each with a distinct character, providing guests an exclusive, luxurious experience while maintaining a connection to the land and its history.

Under Gabby's approval and guidance, along with Gio's working energy, La Terre Felice thrived. The *agriturismo* blended the warmth of a family-run establishment with the elegance of a world-class retreat. As word spread, La Terre Felice gained recognition as one of Italy's top destinations, thanks to the captivating storytelling of writer Gio Marzo.

Gabby beamed with immense pride and joy when she saw what Gio had accomplished. Though her remission was a blessing, it was temporary, and she cherished every moment she had to witness La Terre Felice's further transformation.

Gio discovered his role in the world, a family, and the fact that what he searched for in his travels was always there for him to take.

For a while, everything was aligning as Gabby and Gio's aspirations came to life in the success of La Terre Felice.

Chapter 35

Life's Back Nine

As La Terre Felice exploded in recognition, Gio was called to Venice to accept a prestigious writing award for his work, positioning the *agriturismo* as a five-star international travel destination. The award was a testament to all they had achieved together, and Gabby was thrilled that their efforts were being recognized on such a grand scale.

Despite the honor, Gio was reluctant to leave. Gabby was still recovering, and despite Gio's wish for her to be there by his side, she was not up for the travel and fanfare that would zap her energy. Tending to her guests was where she wanted to be at all times.

After Gio's last return to La Terre Felice, he couldn't shake that his place was there with Gabby. But Gabby, ever the supportive partner, insisted that he go. She believed this award would put the final seal of approval on all they had built as a team.

"This is for all of us," Gabby told Gio with a smile, her eyes filled with pride. "Go. Accept it. It's the recognition we've worked so hard for."

Reluctantly, Gio agreed, trusting Gabby's instincts this time. He promised to return as soon as possible and to set a new wedding date, not wanting to be separated any longer than necessary.

The event in Venice was a whirlwind—filled with speeches, media interviews, and accolades.

"I accept this award on behalf of Gabriella and Antoinette Rosetti and the team," Gio said. "They are the heart and soul of La Terre Felice."

Gio's thoughts were of Gabby back in Tuscany. Her illness became a silent struggle, one that she bore with quiet dignity, never wanting to cause undue worry for those around her, especially Antoinette. But as her condition worsened, it became apparent that the collective impact of her disease would be fatal.

Gabby's compromised immune system increasingly impacted her body's ability to protect vital organs like her heart and liver. In addition, neurological issues surfaced that further weakened her strength and stamina to handle basic daily work. Gabby was forced to rest more often during each day.

In the final stages, the autoimmune disease left Gabby frail and exhausted. Her body could no longer mount a defense against even the most minor infections, and every setback became a battle for her life. Although Gabby never gave up hope, the reality of her condition was apparent. Her once vibrant presence at La Terre Felice was fading. Her time was limited.

Gio flew home as soon as the award festivities were over, eager to share the moment with Gabby and see the joy on her face when he placed the award in her hands. But when he arrived at La Terre Felice, the atmosphere was different. The usually vibrant *agriturismo* was heavy with an unfamiliar silence.

Franco, ever the companion soulmate called by Antoinette, broke the news.

"Gabby passed away while resting earlier just today," he said somberly. "She passed peacefully, surrounded by the love and warmth of the home and the people she cherished. It was as if she had waited for you to go, Gio, to accept the award that symbolized the culmination of your dreams, before letting go."

The news hit Gio like a tidal wave, drowning him in a sea of emotions—grief, regret, and an overwhelming sense of loss. He had been so close, yet again away when Gabby needed him most. The award, a symbol of their success, now seemed hollow in her absence.

But as the initial shock subsided, Gio realized that Gabby had given him a final gift. She ensured that he was not burdened with the pain of witnessing her final moments, allowing him to remember her as strong, determined, vibrant, and full of life. She orchestrated everything, as she always had, with wisdom beyond words.

Gio stood alone in the quiet of La Terre Felice, the place that had become their shared legacy, now emptier than ever. Yet, in that emptiness, Gabby's presence was there—her spirit woven into the fabric of the land they had nurtured together. With a bittersweet certainty, Gio knew that Gabby's spirit would always be a part of La Terre Felice and him.

Chapter 36

Celebration and Discovery

Gio continued to stare at Gabby's image back in the hotel room at the Grand Timeo. He sat silently, deep in thought going over the past few years and his unique, complicated relationship with Gabby.

The room was dark, and the only light came from Mount Etna's fiery orange and red hues. The iconic volcano graced Taormina's view and decided to erupt once again. But at that moment, the eruption only played background noise to the void inside Gio's heart.

Gio's mind was a storm of emotions. The reality of Gabby's passing had yet to sink in. As he gazed at the urn on the credenza, he sensed floating in a dreamlike trance, disconnected from everything around him.

He recalled his introduction to Gabby in San Gimi, when they talked for hours and days, getting to know one another, their zest for life, food, the arts, and enthusiastic lovemaking under the stars. How could he …

A knock at the hotel room door startled Gio, pulling him out of his thoughts. He hesitated, unsure if he even wanted to face anyone. But then he remembered where and why he was there and rose to answer.

When he opened the door, Franco stood there, his expression a mixture of sadness and solidarity. Without a word, Franco stepped inside and pulled Gio into a firm embrace.

The two men remained there for a long moment, connected by friendship, combined experiences, shared grief, and deep bond with Gabby.

"I'm here to take you to the gathering," Franco said, his voice thick with emotion. "We'll honor her, Gio. The way she wanted."

Gio nodded, unable to find the words to respond. Together, they left the room and went to the celebration of Gabby's life.

The event displayed everything Gabby cherished—tradition and elegance, infused with Tuscan warmth, people, and beauty. It brought together friends, family, and all those lives touched by her work at La Terre Felice.

As guests moved about, the weight of the occasion pressed down on Gio. Yet, a comforting sense of peace embraced him, as if Gabby's spirit was present, woven into the very essence of the life she loved. The celebration mirrored her. It was filled with love, laughter, and a profound appreciation for the simple pleasures of Italy.

Among the crowd, Gio was shocked to see his mother, Isabella Maranzzano, who had been invited to the celebration by Antoinette. Gabby's mamma felt it was time for Gio to reconnect with his family again, with a true love that only a mother can understand and provide.

When Isabella looked up and saw her son, her face lighting up with delight. "Gio? Is that you?" she exclaimed, rushing forward to embrace her son.

Gio returned his mother's hug, a surge of emotion welling within him. "Yes, Mamma. I am so glad you are here."

Tears of joy glistened in Isabella's eyes as she accompanied Gio through the gathering. Despite the awkwardness and the passage of time, Italian blood and history still ran deep.

When it was Gio's turn to speak, he stood before the crowd with Gabby spiritually next to him, his voice quivering. Without leaving his mother's eyes, he told stories of Gabby's strength, passion for La Terre Felice, and love for everyone who entered the estate.

"Gabby was a bright and beautiful shining star," Gio began. "She loved the estate and the people who worked there, and she treated all guests as equals. Her beauty was stunning, yet her soulful aura was what captivated me the first time our eyes locked. I miss Gabby terribly."

Gio reflected on Gabby's dreams, her vision, and how she had shown him the true meaning of love—not only for a person, but for a place, its people, a way of life, and the land that had become their legacy.

"I only truly realized what home meant after Gabby was gone," Gio admitted, trembling. "But Tuscany, La Terre Felice, the traditions, and the experience of loving those things will hold Gabby in my heart forever. La Terre Felice was her dream, and it's now my duty, my promise before her, to keep it running well, to support Antoinette, and to ensure the legacy Gabby built lives on."

Gio paused, gazing at the faces before him, each united by their love for Gabby. "La Terre Felice is a part of me now. And through it, Gabby will always be honored and remembered. She was the love of my life."

After the celebration, Gio returned with Gabby's ashes to La Terre Felice. He and Franco strolled through the vineyards, olive groves, and gardens that had always been Gabby's pride and joy.

Standing on the hill overlooking the *agriturismo*, Gio said, "You are my witness, Franco. I vow to continue Gabby's dream—to care for the land she cherished and to honor her memory in every decision we make."

Gio understood the journey ahead would be challenging. The ache of losing Gabby would linger forever. But he also found his true purpose, rooted in the soil of Tuscany, in the comfort of being Italian and in the love Gabby had shown him.

Moved by the reconnection with his mother, Gio asked Antoinette's permission to invite

Isabella to stay at La Terre Felice. Because Isabella was now nearing retirement age, getting away from the unsettled weather of the Northeast United States would suit her well. This was also the right time for Gio to reconnect with his roots and embrace what once defined his sense of belonging. He realized home is not an image or a far-off land, but the people, culture, and traditions that make it meaningful.

Looking out over the rolling hills, Gio recognized his deep connection to everything Gabby had nourished. It was an association that would carry her by his side and in his soul forever, a love that would guide him for the rest of his days.

With a heavy but determined heart, Gio turned to Franco, Antoinette, and Isabella, who joined them on the hill. "We'll keep it going," he said, his voice steady, his eyes turning up. "For you, Gabby. For all of us."

As the Tuscan sun dropped over La Terre Felice, Gio knew he would never be alone. With Franco, Antoinette, and Isabella embracing him, he said to himself, *Ciao, Amore Mio. We're home.*

Va' pensiero, sull'ali dorate…

Cross the mountains and fly

Over the oceans.

Reach the land, find the place where all children go,

Every night after listening to this lullaby …

Epilogue

Twilight in San Gimignano

The evening sky was about to outline one of the many towers in San Gimignano, Italy. The little jewel on a hilltop in Tuscany, San Gimi, is surrounded by cypress-dotted hillsides mixed in with row after row of olive trees and grape vines all painting the lush landscape of the Val d'Elsa. Located a stone's throw from Renaissance Florence, this is an epicenter of today's modern Italian world.

As I grab an outdoor table at a taverna in Piazza della Cisterna, I can almost take a bite out of the aroma of fresh basil. My favorite dish—manicotti—was being prepared along with fresh bread steaming from the oven and a bottle of the region's best *vino rosso*. Right here and now, this is where I belonged.

After three visits to the motherland and exploring more cities than I can count, it's time to unwind in this Italian paradise and reflect on the adventure that's been a lifetime in the making.

The research, the writing, the sights, sounds, and people—all of it was wonderful. But now, as the bells of the Duomo begin their evening song, my thoughts drift, and I wonder, *How did I end up here?*

For as long as I can remember, I could put pen to paper and now fingers to keys. Even at the university, I preferred the finesse of an essay to the multiple-guess disaster any day of the week.

Authoring a book was all I wanted to do. But what was marketable? What genre would sell in this crazy world of lightning-paced, virtual attention spans? Was it political intrigue? Sports? Or heaven forbid healthcare, which I knew enough about to be dangerous?

No, it was none of that, and I'll tell you why. Sometimes the best stories are from the heart—something that lives within your experiences to connect the past to the present and reflect ahead. It strikes a chord with many of us in this generation looking to leave a mark or a legacy.

Idealistic? Perhaps. Realistic? Yes. It turned out to be the winning formula.

The idea was finalized, and Gio's quest for self-discovery came alive—to again own his Italian heritage. It was easy. After all, I am living it.

The fictional 'real'? Gio Marzo was a third-generation Italian, who after being embarrassed and mocked as a young boy for his ethnicity, realized almost too late what he missed by not embracing his Italian birthright many years ago.

Much later in life, he revisited his family history, learned to speak some Italian, and traveled to the many cultural sites that he finally rediscovered as his home. Now, as a proud Italian, he hoped to come to peace with his ancestry before leaving this Earth.

Thinking about *my* life, with all the advantages I've enjoyed after a successful career, the pressure of today's work environment is nothing compared to what my grandfather endured during his early life. He came to America as a young man, a passenger on a steamer ship that navigated the Atlantic and arrived at Ellis Island in 1913. My grandfather didn't speak English, but he gained comfort and sponsorship from a brother who preceded him. He and his brother Giuseppe worked as stone masons well into their eighties, and as men of few words they didn't communicate much to each other driving together each day. They built hand-cut stone houses and churches, a few of which are still standing today in small towns in Pennsylvania and New Jersey. This was worth retelling, and it's referenced as part of Gio's heritage in this book. My grandfather and his brother were two of many proud people who immigrated to America in the early 20th century. Despite their ongoing challenges, they helped build the industrial foundation of the United States.

Knowing my character Gio was just a by-product of that heritage, I had to embrace the character who like many first-borns of my generation struggled to find their way through life.

"Signor Gio, your phone. It's buzzing." My daydream is interrupted by the taverna's waiter, Aldo. I think, *Who would be ringing me in this part of the world?*

"*Ciao. Si...Si...(a long pause) Incredibile! Tante grazie. Ciao, ciao, arrivederci.*"

It was my editor/agent on the call. There's potential to become a publishing top-seller in contemporary fiction, and who knows what else...the *New York Times* list? A movie? Do I dare to dream big?

Like others, I published this novella independently to maximize the release. It's a bit surreal. The fictional manuscript is now published, and the genre, like many first-time authors, incorporates much truth in the characters portrayed.

If there's a chance *Ciao, Amore Mio* becomes a top seller, then wine for everyone!

The air is alive in San Gimi. The bells continue their chant, breaking into the still night, and I have come full circle.

The birthright is intact.

My grandfather would be so proud.

Acknowledgments

A story cannot be told without characters. Much of this novella is based on people and situations in life. Thank you for your support and encouragement to all of the people who suffered through my early writing.

Thank you to my high school teachers, who encouraged me to write for the school newspaper. I balked at the offer. I was a jock and didn't think it was cool enough. I always remember that missed opportunity.

To my grandparents, Giovanni Sr. and Madeline, you inspired me to rediscover my Italian heritage. I'm sorry now for not embracing the language as a boy and for asking you to speak in English. My biggest regret was not becoming fluent in Italian.

My grandmother would always remind me to "be good for Nonna." I hope I lived up to that in this life. My grandfather was something else. Whenever I walked in the door for a visit, he would proclaim, "Prince of Wales, Prince of Wales." That was a reference, of course, to Prince Charles of England, who was a young man at that time.

To my parents, John Jr. and Rose, who demanded I learn in school and who provided for our family. We didn't have much, but were still taught a value system of right from wrong and encouraged to embrace opportunity.

To my Aunt Dot, a rebel teenager in her day, who took me under her wing and continues to support me to this day.

To my sister, Cathy, the keeper of our family history, who with her husband, Mark, raised two boys now contributing to the world.

To Jamie, my wife of forty years, it's been a wonderful journey shared—*Amore Totale* for putting up with me this long and for your instincts about life.

Other friends and golfing buds who deserve a mention are Tony Karam, thanks for pushing me to incorporate more intrigue into this novella, and, Mike Kopp, the original Coach K, who is always supportive and the most positive person I know. Plus, Larry Bonner is a character extraordinaire who is full of ideas for this group. Where would we be without an idea man?

Thanks to my editor and publisher, Jennifer Bright of Bright Communications, and my cover designer, Nancy McLaughlin of Sky Design.

To Tuscany, Sicily, and all parts of the motherland: She is flawed and stuck in time. That's the beauty of Italy. Going back to traditions lost. A clear brand attribute and why so many people from around the world visit each year. Thanks for the experience of a lifetime.

Finally, I must mention Larry Pastorius, who lists his LinkedIn profile as "Traveler." In the summer of '74, we partied together a lot while attempting to finish our undergraduate work at Bloomsburg University. Somehow we both made it.

Recently, Larry sent me a note on his way to Cortona, Italy, reminding me to include Amelita Galli-Curci, the most famous Italian opera singer of the twentieth century, in my story. I did, Larry. Thank you!

About the Author

J.A. Marz began his career as a recreation executive for an inner-city youth organization and then as a sports journalist for a daily newspaper in Eastern Pennsylvania before transitioning into the healthcare industry as a communications professional.

Although now retired from healthcare, J.A. served as a chief marketing officer for various health networks and implemented new business strategies in the industry for more than twenty-five years.

He was among the first to coin the term "Moneyball Marketing" in the healthcare world, highlighting the importance of demonstrating value and return on investment. J.A. also has experience in crisis communication and is well-versed in performance metrics, promotion, sports marketing, and hospitality.

Writing and storytelling have always been J.A.'s passion, along with golf, travel, music, and all things Italy. He is excited to publish work that touches the soul. This marks his first published book.

J.A. holds a Bachelor of Arts degree from Bloomsburg University in Pennsylvania and earned an Executive Leadership certificate from Georgetown University's Center for Professional Development in Washington, DC.